A Fateful Flaw

The 40-Day Wilderness Journey of Jesus

A Novel

Larry Moeller

Warning

This work contains adult content, whimsy, and humor. At times it strays from biblical tradition and may therefore be provocative. Not intended for academic consumption.

ISBN 978-1-63814-587-5 (Paperback)
ISBN 978-1-63814-589-9 (Hardcover)
ISBN 978-1-63814-588-2 (Digital)

Covenant Books
11661 Hwy 707
Murrells Inlet, SC 29576
www.covenantbooks.com

Reactions Across Christian Traditions

Episcopal. *Haven't we all wondered what happened with Jesus in the desert? This colorful and intriguing novel will help you to expand your imaginings. Most importantly, it will help you to reexamine God's plan for us through Jesus. Enjoy!* Bonnie Anders. Church home: St. Elizabeth Episcopal Church, Farragut, Tennessee.

Wesleyan. *The author brings a wonderful flair to Jesus's forty-day journey in the desert and sparks the imagination of the reader in its well-written style. This work provides an interesting new perspective of what Jesus went through for the salvation of the world.* Rev. Dr. Philip Stevenson, District Superintendent. Church home: Spring Valley Church, Rocklin, California.

Presbyterian. *You will imagine Jesus's encounters with the devil in ways you may not have considered. Through conversational inquiry and thoughtful reflection, the author transcends time, bringing the past into the present to instill hope for the future: the promise of God for all humanity. It is a delightful and intriguing theological challenge.* Cathy Monkman, CCE. Church home: Covenant Presbyterian Church, San Antonio, Texas.

Nondenominational. *When you decide to stand for God and His principles, you had better expect a storm. The good news is that Father God always joins us in the midst of that storm. This is a wonderful read that triggers thought and reflection and reaffirms one's faith.* Carol Collins. Church home: Lakewood Church, Houston, Texas.

Roman Catholic. *An intriguing exploration of the trials and challenges we all face in our daily lives and faith journey. The vivid detail and illustration of Jesus's humanity affirm it is okay to doubt and regret actions we take in exercising our free will—and later come to terms with those actions.* Gerry Ferguson. Church home: Holy Name of Jesus, Harrisburg, Pennsylvania

African Methodist Episcopal (AME). *The imagery made my senses explode, a provocative and challenging read which forced me to reconcile Jesus's humanity in ways I had never thought about before.* Keira Wyatt. Church home: Greater Warner Tabernacle A.M.E. Zion, Knoxville, Tennessee.

Seventh Day Adventist (SDA). *The personal impassioned force in my Christian faith is to scream the message of God's love for all, especially when it comes to His enemy. A Fateful Flaw screams it loudly. It's a page turner!* Tulio Robinson. Church home: Maryville Seventh Day Adventist Church, Maryville, Tennessee.

Baptist. *Very thought provoking, with a perfect swirl of biblical facts and fantasy, evoking emotions of sadness, humor, empathy, love…and most importantly, hope.* Lori Hogan. Church home: Gatewood Baptist Church, Fayetteville, West Virginia.

Lutheran. *If you are looking for orthodox or easy theology, you won't find it in this fictionalized recounting of Jesus's temptation; that is most certainly not the author's intent. For centuries, biblical theologians have done plenty of speculating on that. What you will find in this imaginative work are probing questions about Jesus's mission and how in these forty days of temptation, Jesus comes to understand and accept that mission.* Rev. H. Julian Gordy. Bishop Emeritus, ELCA Southeastern Synod.

Other Books by the Author

Claim the Flame
A Series of Seven Two-Character Dialogues Featuring the Apostle
Paul and His First-Century Church Contemporaries
© 2015 by Larry Moeller

The Query
What is the Reason for the Hope that is Within You?
© 2016 by Larry Moeller

To honor and remember

All whose lives ended unexpectedly because of the coronavirus—
and especially neighbor Paula,
who succumbed at home on Christmas Eve

CONTENTS

PREFACE

It happened in those days that Jesus came from Nazareth of Galilee and was baptized in the Jordan by John. On coming up out of the water, he saw the heavens being torn open and the Spirit, like a dove, descending upon him. And a voice came from the heavens, *You are my beloved Son; with you I am well pleased.* At once the Spirit drove him out into the desert, and he remained in the desert for forty days, tempted by Satan. He was among wild beasts and the angels ministered to him.

—Mark 1:9–13 (NAB)

INTRODUCTION

What really happened during the forty days in the wilderness? Scripture provides scant insight. Following his baptism, Jesus is whisked away into the desert wilderness for a time of—what? Of contemplation, perhaps. Or reflection—reflection on the trajectory of humanity from the moment of creation. Or preparation—preparation for a ministry which would consume him and alter that trajectory.

Timeline

This fictional work fills in the gaps. It begins with Day 0—the day before the baptism—when the Archangel Michael engages the satan. Jesus's journey begins the next day, Day 1, following the descent of the Spirit upon him.

Biblical Tradition

A majority of contemporary biblical scholars hold that the Gospel of Mark was the first to be written, perhaps thirty years after Jesus's death. The Gospels of Matthew and Luke follow a decade or two later, while the fourth Gospel (John) appears toward the end of the first century CE. None of the gospels suggest Jesus's interaction during the forty-day journey with ancestors of his faith. Accordingly, these dialogues depart from biblical tradition.

Human or Divine

Was Jesus both human *and* divine? The answer has been debated by theologians for centuries. Perhaps with the baptismal indwelling of the Spirit, the man Jesus began living into that divinity. Could the forty days have been a time for him to navigate this dual-yet-one identity? If so, might there have been bumps along the way—sometimes seemingly more human than divine, at other times more divine than human? That is the tension in the character of Jesus encountered here.

Context and Footnotes

To offer biblical context to story segments, related Scripture passages are designated by footnotes; for convenience, the full texts comprise the Appendix. As the initial footnote example, Scripture does provide insight on Jesus's nature as both human and divine.[1]

Style and Purpose

Throughout, humor interlaces fantasy with possibility. By intimate interaction among historical characters, the man Jesus explores the gift of free will in the nature of humanity, probes the insidious effect of temptation to alter the course of one's life, and confronts the very essence of the satan himself.

In the forty days, clarity of purpose comes.

---

[1] Philippians 2:5–8a

DAY 0

Michael and the Satan
The Beckoning

No one had ever been here. Long ago, life had tried. Sage, grass, and trees had tried—and long ago died. In the midst of the vast desert wilderness, the naked, twisted, beaten skeleton of an ancient oak stood withered under the cloudless sky—a petrified witness to the ageless ravages of the searing heat.

From far off, the contrast made him noticeable. He was draped in a dark cloak hung loosely from the shoulders to the sand at his feet. It was the cloak that stood in contrast to the desert emptiness and the lifeless sentinel a hundred paces away. He was erect and alone, pondering the ancient oak in the silence of the arid heat, with no sign of how he had come or how long he had been. He was waiting.

Hours passed. An occasional breeze brought life to the folds of his cloak. But he remained still, determined. He was waiting. The emptiness would soon change. His gaze turned toward the sound of a distant rumble. A dark-silver thread was stretching across the horizon. Nothing would stand in the way of the advancing storm. The wait was over. It swept quickly across the emptiness. Towering blackness shook as lightning bolts danced. Driven sand darkened the sky; thunder roared. In the midst of the biting wind, the stinging sand, and the deafening roar, the standing one was determined, dark cloak flailing behind. Time seemed to stop as the heightening storm swirled about him. But he was unmoved.

"Who sent you to this place?" a voice at last thundered above the roar.

The resolute one remained unmoved, silent. The storm intensified.

"Why are you here?" the voice thundered again, more loudly to best the angry storm. Wind-driven sand and rocks pounded relentlessly from all around, yet the standing one stood unmoved and silent as the fury grew. "Who are you?" the voice boomed as the ground trembled. "What do you want? Why are you here?" The power of the storm sent rocks and boulders flying, while the sand swirled with such intensity no ordinary man could stand.

"You know who I am!" the standing one shouted against the storm. "And because you know who I am, you know who sent me!" The declaration reverberated against the towering thunderheads: "You know who sent me," it repeated, over and over. "You know who sent me. You know who sent me." Again and again and again: "You know who sent me!"

Beneath the deafening roar, an eerie guttural moan slowly grew until its intensity matched that of the raging storm. It was as though all the anger of time had focused in this place. All destructive powers gathered and unleashed in this moment upon the standing one! Yet he remained unmoved and unscathed—upright and purposeful.

"Why…are…you…here?" the voice shrieked with a power that echoed through time.

Oblivious to the fury, he turned and set his gaze in the direction from which the voice had come. As though following his gaze, the swirling center shifted. In its midst, the image of a second man slowly emerged from behind the trunk of the unscathed tree as the storm intensity lessened. Soon the serenity of the barren landscape surrounded them in the desert calm.

Similarities were immediately apparent. Conviction underscored their gaze as each sized up the other. Determination creased their strong brows. Certainty set their jaws. Yes, their common lineage was apparent. Yet there were notable differences. Historic differences.

The appearance of outward calm belied his inner turmoil. He was dressed comfortably, suggesting an interruption to an otherwise casual summer afternoon. The open linen shirt, loin wrap, and sandals complemented his natural bronze. Yet the fury of the storm seethed just beneath the surface as muscles in arms and legs pulsed. He was ready for whatever the visitor would bring.

"I don't want you here, Michael," the stormy one hissed! "You know this place is mine, and you know you are not welcome." The anger was deep seated, evident in the clenched jaw and hardened glare from the steel-gray eyes. "So why are you here?" he demanded. There was something about Michael that always put the stormy one off balance, which is why he despised him so. The hatred was deeply rooted and, he felt, deserved. It hadn't always been that way, but it was now.

Michael wasn't looking forward to this visit. Since the beginning, he had encountered and endured the wrath of the stormy one many times. Far too many times. Yet he was always the one who was sent. These visits were never pleasant, but the fury-filled greeting and the hatred in the cold stare made it clear that this one especially would not go well. He met the stare with the same intensity. "Nice welcome," Michael began with a touch of defiance. "What do they call you these days? I've lost track..."

"You're not going to be here long enough to call me anything," the stormy one sneered, "so get on with it." His eyes narrowed. "Why...are...you...here?" he bellowed. Hatred was consuming him.

"How about *Storm*? That seems appropriate. I'll call you *Storm* this time," Michael said as he ignored the question and turned aside. He paused as his eyes scanned the landscape. "I can see why it was this place. It all makes sense. I Am didn't want any distractions."

"What's that supposed to mean?" Storm sneered.

"It feels different," Michael continued, ignoring Storm's question. "Stepping into the realm of time always feels different, but this time..." his voice trailed off as he turned slowly and absorbed the desolation. "'No distractions,' I Am had said. 'No distractions.' I see now. No breath of life. No creatures. No humans." Michael's gaze slowly fixed on Storm. Then quietly, he slowly repeated, "No distractions."

Storm's eyes narrowed, seething hatred. "Why…are…you… here?" he hissed coldly. "What…do…you…want?" he hissed more forcefully as rage consumed him. "This…is…*my*…realm," he seethed. The ground shook, the wind roared. Sand swirled about them. "You…do…not…belong…here," Storm bellowed, his face and body contorted in hate.

Michael was unmoved and waited for the fury to subside. "I'm a messenger," he declared. "I Am wants to see you…here…as a man. He knows you've been watching, and he knows you are curious. He will meet you…here. In eight days. That is why I have come. I Am sent me."

"Why?" Storm bellowed. "What does he want?"

"I'm just the messenger, Storm," Michael said as he turned to leave. "Just the messenger. You will soon know what he wants." And as silently as he had come, Michael departed.

DAY 1

Jesus and Michael
Baptism and the Heavenly Hosts

"It's time, Michael. It is time."

Michael had never understood. Why had I Am created time and wrapped the earthly wonder within its bounds? In the beginning, all of creation was in harmony—the heavenly hosts and earthly beings—all in harmony, unfettered. Yes, the earthly ones were created for I Am's pleasure in the earthly domain, and the heavenly ones for I Am's limitless pleasure. But why time? Why this burden for the earthly ones? Why the shackles of time on earth? Michael had never understood.

But here, I Am—the God of all that was and is to come—here at this moment, is bound by time.

"I don't understand," Michael said. "I have never understood."

"Yes, I know," I Am replied softly.

When I Am decided to submit to the tether of time, Michael and all the heavenly hosts were mystified—though excited—about the privilege of serving as earthly protectors to the newborn Jesus. They had shared in delight of his toddler wonder, in awe of the quiet tenderness of the nurturing mother, and in admiration of the gentle firmness of the teaching father. They thrilled as Jesus grew in knowledge and understanding of the mystery of I Am. When all around were confounded, he was enlightened.

John knew. For as long as he could remember, John had sensed an air of divine purpose around his cousin—Jesus. So it had come as no surprise on this day at the Jordan when Jesus insisted on baptism.[2] John knew. John knew it was time, time to set in motion the purpose for which Jesus had come. When the heavens opened, and I Am's essence filled the man Jesus, John knew. From that moment, the shackles of time had been altered. The world didn't know, though John knew. So did Michael. And so did Storm. At that moment, the fullness of I Am stepped into Storm's earthly realm in the man, Jesus—a man shackled by time. Something had changed. Something was changing. Only I Am knew.

"You have served well." I Am smiled as he glanced around at the life which surrounded him in the midst of the desolation. Michael and the heavenly hosts now in earthly form—creatures and people of all sorts—were dancing and tumbling with joy. The jubilant song of all creation had returned and was now a symphony of exultant celebration.

Just a moment earlier in heavenly form, they had witnessed the man Jesus approach John and ask to be baptized. The river had been teeming with people young and old as one by one, John had cleansed them in the waters of the slow-moving Jordan.

"Wash me," Jesus had said to John as he approached.

John knew. "I need to be washed by you," he had observed, "yet you come to me for washing?"

"It is time," Jesus had declared. "Now is the time."

The eyes of those on the shore had been fixed in merriment on all those frolicking in the river who had been cleansed. No one else had been attentive to the intimate conversation between the cousins standing on the shore. Together they had waded into the waters. The ritual cleansing. The parting of the sky. The voice. A heavenly being descending. Gone.

"You have served well, Michael," I Am repeated, eyes dancing around with delight. The sounds of jubilation rose and echoed across the desolate distance. "You have served well, and you will serve well

---

[2] Matthew 3:13–15

in this place in the days to come." The sense of peace and joy flowed from I AM as the celebration grew. Life was all around; the desolation receded. Abundant life had returned, overflowing with the song of creation. And the joy of the celebration became one with the peace of I AM.

I AM turned to the cloaked one. "Walk with me." He beckoned as he slowly made his way through the new life around them.

It was peculiar, Michael thought, *almost bizarre*. Why would the All Powerful enter time in the person of a simple, unassuming man? For sure, the boy-become-man was clearly favored by all who knew him. He was dutiful, with an engaging smile and soft brown eyes that drew others to him. His gaze was gentle, yet deep. He carried an air of humble self-assurance, a confidence learned at the carpenter's bench.

Maybe the simple sand-colored tunic gathered at the waist with a single cord explained why he had gone unnoticed at the river. *It was all very peculiar*, thought Michael as he followed. They walked quietly for a time, I AM clearly enjoying all that was around. There had been a place like this once, Michael recalled.[3] I AM had breathed. There had been a place like this. Yet for reasons beyond Michael's understanding, it had changed. It had changed when time entered the earthly realm.

And now Michael found himself walking with I AM, alongside the man, Jesus. "Name him Jesus," the man who would become his earthly father had been told, "because he will save his people."[4] Michael had been the messenger then too. He had delivered the message. But what was in the mind of I AM? He didn't understand then. He didn't understand yesterday. He didn't understand now.

"I will enjoy this day, Michael…this place. For one day, I will enjoy all that surrounds me. But there is a purpose in what lies ahead. That is why we are here. It is time. To sharpen my thinking and preparation, I will devote the next two days in solitude near the distant outcropping with only water to sustain me. Then the next day,

---

[3] Genesis 2:8–9
[4] Matthew 1:21

I wish to spend time with Moses and Elijah. Tell them to meet me here at midday in human form. You have served well, Michael." He smiled.

DAYS 2, 3

Jesus
Solitude and Fasting

With only a flask of water, Jesus left before dawn.

Maybe he needs time to fully grasp the nature of divine yet human, Michael thought. When the Spirit descended upon him as he came out of the Jordan, it seemed Jesus had changed.

So Michael and the heavenly hosts, together with the wild beasts, waited.

DAY 4

Moses and Elijah
Return to Time

Three were gathered in the shade of the solitary tree, its lush canopy in contrast to the arid desolation all around. Was it the cool spring water at their feet which had their attention? Or the bright-colored fruit within their grasp overhead? They were enjoying the cool serenity in the midst of the desert emptiness.

"You said midday—right, Michael?" he asked with a quick glance to the cloaked one. "You said he would meet us here at midday?" He was bronzed and muscular with firm features and gray eyes. His hair was dark, curly, and well-tended with a beard to match. The voice was confident, with an air of impatience. He was admiring the shade of the canopy surrounding them. "It's midday. Are you sure he meant today? Maybe you were confused." He turned to Michael. "If it was today, where is he?"

"Oh, for the sake of all that is, Moses, give it a rest!" the other exclaimed. "You've been testy since the moment we got here. You know Michael. If I Am told him to meet us here at midday, then we are where we're supposed to be. Give him a break."

"Well, it feels strange to be here, wrapped in time again," Moses replied. "Very strange. It brings back memories, especially in the middle of this desert. I don't understand why I Am would pick a place like this. I spent most of my life in the desert, so it feels strange to be back. At least we have a little shade and some water, so there's that, I guess."

Michael was studying the horizon. "He'll be here. Jesus will come. I've done my part, and that wasn't so easy," he said, turning to Moses with a grin. "Sometimes you can be a little stubborn! With that stubborn streak, it always mystified me why I AM picked you to lead the chosen.[5] But then," he continued, turning back to the horizon, "there's a lot I don't understand. Anyway, he told me to call him Jesus during his time here. You too."

"I wonder why he wants *me* here?" the other asked. "I came into time generations after Moses. I wonder what Jesus is thinking?" He was stocky, the shortest of the three. Graying hair swept his shoulders, complemented by the flowing beard. The crimson silk tunic with golden sash contrasted a quiet confidence. His manner bespoke calm, unlike the brash Moses.

"Jesus knows, Elijah," Michael reflected. "He knows, and you will soon know too. We all will. For now, we wait."

"Well, while we're waiting," said Moses as he sized up Elijah, "There's something I've wondered about ever since you came into the earthly realm. First though, nice threads." He smirked. "They remind me of when I was favored by the daughter of the pharaoh."[6]

"And what did you wonder about?" Elijah asked, ignoring the smirk. "What was it that caught your eye as you watched from the heavenly realm? Surely not my clothes."

"No, not the flair for clothes. It was more about the powers you received from I AM. It seemed you could claim those powers whenever you wanted—almost without limit." Moses turned. "Now there's something I don't understand, Michael. I don't understand why I received power for a specific purpose but only when it pleased I AM. It wasn't so with him," nodding toward Elijah. "He was free to use the divine powers at will.

"It just seems that I AM kept me on a tight leash but not you," he said to Elijah. "I have always wondered about that. It sure would

---

[5] Exodus 3:11–14
[6] Exodus 2:10

have made it a lot easier to lead if I could have slipped in some little miracles along the way. Why do you think I Aᴍ favored you over me?"

"Maybe it was the clothes," Elijah cackled.

"Well, Moses, you can soon ask him yourself if you want," Michael said. "I don't know why Jesus asked me to bring you here, but I don't think it's about clothes or I Aᴍ 's ways in the earthly realm during your days here. Jesus didn't say. And I don't wonder about those things. But I admit to being confused. Why would I Aᴍ assume the form of a human and shackle himself with time? These things mystify me."

It was the faint yelp that caught them short. In the distance, a young jackal frolicked in a cloud of dust about the solitary man slowly approaching. The desert falcon at rest on his shoulder suddenly leaped into the air, sending the jackal into a frenzy. It swooped in taunting ever-widening circles just above the reach of the frenzied leaps and snapping jaws—then back to his shoulder. Laughter filled the air. It was a game with the man, the jackal, and the falcon fully engaged. As he drew nearer, they soon joined the laughter over the jackal and falcon at play.

"You are enjoying yourself," Michael called. "Some new friends?"

The jackal turned to the strange voice and bounded across the desert sand, heading straight for the cloaked one. Almost upon him, it sprang into the air. Narrowly missing Michael, it sailed past and splashed with abandon into the spring-fed pool. It had found a new game while the falcon found peace in the leaf-laden tree.

"Pure delight!" Jesus exclaimed, his feet covered with dust, his brow glistening in the desert heat. "Creatures at play. Is anything more beautiful?" he asked, eyes smiling.

"Well, on a day like today, a little shade and some cool spring water is right up there," observed Moses. The laughter continued as the jackal flopped lazily in the middle of the pool and fell still.

"Indeed," said Jesus. "She's been nonstop for the past hour. The cool water sounds good." He waded into the pool. "Have you tried the fruit?" He glanced overhead.

"No," Michael said. "We've been waiting." He picked a couple of apples, a pear, and a nectarine from the tree. "We'll join you." He sat at the edge with his feet in the water. "This does feel good!"

"Come, Moses...and Elijah," Jesus beckoned as he cupped has hand and drank, then stretched out beside Michael at the water's edge. "Make yourselves comfortable and enjoy some fruit."

Elijah hesitated and looked about, while Moses took the pear from Michael's outstretched hand and sat down.

"The water of a desert spring," Moses sighed. "There is nothing more refreshing."

Elijah's anxiety was evident.

"Is everything all right?" Jesus asked, looking at Elijah. "Has returning to the earthly realm been difficult? What troubles you?"

"Nothing a little humility won't cure," Moses jeered. "He just doesn't want to get his fancy clothes dirty!"

In a blink, Elijah sat...and laughter filled the air. Quiet conversation flowed as fruit and cool water refreshed. Elijah and Moses were enjoying Jesus's stories of the human experience. They reveled in the telling of their own stories as question followed question. Clearly, Jesus was searching.

Michael sat as the hours passed—silent, transfixed, and confused. Sensing the discomfort, Jesus turned to him. "You have been silent, Michael. What troubles you?"

"No, not troubled," he replied. "Confused. I simply don't understand. Why, Jesus? Why enter the earthly realm? Why have you submitted yourself to the shackles of time? Why here in human form? And why Moses and Elijah? Why?"

"Patience, Michael, patience," he replied. "The purpose will unfold. It lies ahead."

DAY 5

Michael and Elijah Questions

For most of his thirty years, Jesus had sensed something was missing. Now he knew. Completeness had been missing. In the baptismal waters of the Jordan, fullness had come.

Yet why these two, Michael wondered? *And especially, why Moses?* Like all humans since the garden had been closed to them, Moses had come into time as a helpless baby.[7] As with other infant Hebrew boys, he had been cast aside under Pharaoh's decree. Through his mother's saving act and her love and tenderness, he grew to be favored by those with earthly power—in fact, by the very Pharaoh who had rejected him.

In time, Moses's purpose became clear: to disrupt and to deliver. Still, he resisted. The flaming bush in the desert was his awakening.[8] Slowly, determination became his strength, an unwavering determination to his purpose: to disrupt the enslavement of the nation of Israel under Pharaoh's rule and to deliver them to a land of their own—to deliver the "people of the promise" to the land of promise.

Jesus turned. "Here's what I want to know, Moses. How did you stay true to the purpose, once you understood it? What kept you on

---

7   Exodus 2:1–3
8   Exodus 3:1–2

that path? And how did you persevere when those in power rejected you? Why did you persist so?"

Michael listened intently to the dialogue with Moses, though mystified. Surely Jesus knew. But Jesus's questions were genuine. He wasn't testing Moses. His questions reflected a genuine search for understanding.

"*You're* curious, Jesus?" Moses asked. Moses had slept well and risen early to catch the sunrise. He was fully alert—the early-morning dip in the cool spring water had taken care of that.

"I'm not sure where to go with this," Moses began. "Even though Michael said we are to call you Jesus for now, it is hard for me to see you as only a man. Clearly, if you were only a man, none of us would be here in this place, at this time. Especially Elijah and me. And since we *are* here, it is because of the authority you have over all things, even time. So I'm not sure where to go with this. I don't understand how learning more about how I stayed on the path to deliver God's people serves a purpose. When he beckoned us, Michael said he didn't understand why—only that we were to come. And now your questions confuse even me!"

*****

There is something about this tree, thought Michael. In all the assignments within the realm of time, never had he tasted fruit so luscious, so satisfying. With only a couple of bites, hunger had left. He had watched Elijah gather his tunic in the moonlight and head toward the eastern horizon with the jackal playfully at his side. Moses and Jesus had been fast asleep, but not Michael. It had been a fitful night.

At dawn, he had been transfixed by the low-hanging nectarine. Now only the pit remained. The bits and pieces of quiet conversation between Moses and Jesus didn't compare to the fullness of this fruit. He leaned over the pool and washed the sweet nectar from his hands and drank deeply of the cool water.

Jesus had spread his tunic on the ground and was lying on his side while absorbing the unfolding tale. Moses's telling would take a while, so Michael set out for the far horizon where Elijah had disappeared. The still of the evening was now the still of early morn; the trail in the sand of the jackal and man was undisturbed. Cresting the horizon, a cluster of boulders stood far in the distance. The trail led there.

The boulders were further than first appeared. It was midmorning by the time he arrived. Lying in the shade with the jackal at his feet, Elijah was asleep. The jackal raised its head and turned toward the gentle shuffle of the approaching one. The low, quiet guttural warning roused Elijah; he rolled and followed the jackal's stare.

"Good morning, Michael." Elijah yawned. "I couldn't resist sleeping under the stars with the shadow of these rocks to hold off the rising sun, and I guess our four-footed friend tagged along. It was drawn to the early-morning shade too, it seems. Did Jesus send you?"

"No," Michael replied. "He's been asking questions of Moses, and well, you know Moses. Moses has plenty to share, and heaven knows he's not the quickest storyteller. I have a feeling they'll be busy for a while. So I thought I'd track you down and figured you might be hungry. This nectarine is unbelievable!" He pulled one from his cloak and tossed it to Elijah. "It refreshes, both hunger and thirst. Amazing!"

"Thanks." Elijah smiled. "I *was* starting to get a little hungry, and that's a sensation I've not felt since earthly days." He nibbled slowly on the fruit, savoring each morsel. "What's going on, Michael? What's this all about? What are we doing here?"

"I'm not sure," Michael reflected. "Jesus was asking Moses about how he figured out his purpose and how he stayed true to it. Moses kept rambling off on tangents, so I left. It almost seems that Jesus, this human Jesus, is searching for understanding—and that's where I get confused. He tells me to be patient. And in this earthly form, constrained by time, that is difficult for me. Patience isn't my strong suit!"

"Well, you have been I Am's most loyal and trusted one since before time," Elijah observed. "So whatever I Am is planning, assuming human form as Jesus must be huge. Very huge. It may be that in Jesus, I Am is experiencing some of the traits common to humans—

finding purpose in life, staying true to purpose when so many things distract, whether real or imagined.

"The journey of living can be very difficult, especially when someone decides to trust emotions or desires. Maybe Jesus is wrestling with some of that. He is, after all, human in this time. Maybe that's part of what this is all about. Maybe the human Jesus is wrestling over purpose."

"Maybe so," replied Michael. "Maybe so. Whatever is going on, it must, as you say, be very huge. And somehow in all of it, the fallen one is involved."

"*The fallen one?* You mean the ruler of darkness? The satan?" Elijah's countenance had moved beyond curiosity. "What do you mean *the fallen one is involved?*"

"I don't know how or why," answered Michael. "All I know is a few days ago, I Am sent me to deliver a message to the fallen one. Those assignments are always difficult, and this one especially so. He is always angry with me, but this time, he was *very* angry. I think it was because I had stepped into time. Somehow he believes that time is his domain, that the heavenly beings have no place in his realm. His anger consumed the air and shook the ground. It probably didn't help when I called him *Storm*." Michael grinned.

"*Storm*, huh?" Elijah chuckled. "That was clever. *Storm*. Yeah, I'll bet that set him off. *Storm* is as good a name as any. And in the realm of time—*his realm*, as he claims—well, Storm is so very powerful. Humanity is no match for him." Elijah paused in thought for a moment. Then he asked, "What was the message?"

"The message?" Michael repeated.

"Yes," queried Elijah. "What was the message you delivered? What was the message from I Am which took you there?"

"Oh, it was quite simple really. And certainly not worth all the dramatics," Michael observed. "I just told him that I Am—well, Jesus, actually—would meet him there on Day 8, in a couple of days."

"What else?" Elijah probed, his curiosity piqued. "What else did you tell him?"

"Nothing else," said Michael. "There was nothing else. That was the message—only that. And boy, that set him off! Let's just say, we don't get along. So I got out of there!"

Elijah studied Michael thoughtfully. "Well," he mused absently, "I wonder what this is all about?"

*****

The afternoon had been pleasant, capped by the leisurely return stroll to the spring-fed pool and Tree of Fruit. It was well past dusk when they arrived. All was still in the soft light of the rising moon. Jesus was lying on his side, facing the pond—asleep. The jackal lay curled at his feet with raised head, watching warily as Elijah and Michael found their resting places. Soon the head lowered. It was night—time for rest. Peace settled.

DAY 6

Moses and Elijah
Purpose

The crisp night air would soon give way to the early-morning sun and its warmth. Michael stretched, enjoying the smell and rustle of the soft leaf bed, the source of his restful sleep. Elijah was asleep nearby. Moses, with his low, labored breathing was asleep on the leaves he had carried to the far side of the pool. Jesus and the jackal had disappeared.

He rose slowly, yawned, stretched again, and smiled. These early-morning rituals were one piece of the human experience which always brought delight. The splash of cool spring water on his face was refreshing, as was the satisfying fruit freshly picked.

In the distance, with the light of the approaching dawn, he could see Jesus sitting on the sand in silence, leaning comfortably against a rock. He was alone, eyes closed, facing the rising sun. Michael smiled again, recalling when in Jesus's boyhood, these times of solitude had perplexed his parents—especially his carpenter father, Joseph. The Jerusalem incident—finding his twelve-year-old son in the temple after a frenzied three days—had severely tested Joseph's fatherly patience.[9]

*****

---

[9] Luke 2:41–51

"Of course, I'm proud of him!" he exclaimed as he paced back and forth. He was exasperated, and Mary's soft words in Jesus's defense weren't helping. "Yes, he's a good boy, a good son. But he's going off on his own more and more these days. And now we're going to get home three days later than we planned. That puts me three days behind at the shop—which means three days further behind on the wardrobe I promised Jacob. We're already late on Martha's table. And what about Elizabeth? She's been waiting two months for that storage chest. Pretty soon, Zechariah will be coming by. If we don't keep promises and make deadlines, people will take their business someplace else, and where does that leave us? You don't understand."

"Oh, Joseph," Mary sighed. "He's only twelve and still a boy. Maybe you expect too much of him. I can't think of a single time when he has disobeyed you. Can you? When has he let you down?"

"That's not the point, Mary," Joseph argued, pausing to face her. "He has to remember that we have obligations, and he is a part of those obligations. He has learned well, and I rely on him more and more. Yes, he's only twelve, but I don't expect any more of him than my father expected of me when I was twelve. And I never caused my parents to hunt for me for three days for anything! That's not how a boy becomes a man, and I want my son to be a good man. He can't just wander off on his own, to "debate" or to "think." I depend on him. That's what it means to be a man. To be somebody you can depend on."

Mary sat quietly and reflected on his words. He was a good man, this Joseph, a good father and a caring husband. And she had to admit she was also puzzled by Jesus's behavior. "Maybe he is becoming a man in ways we can't understand, Joseph," she reflected. "Maybe we need to be thinking about how we give him a little freedom while also asking him to respect our needs and wishes too. How often have we remarked that he has an understanding of things which are well beyond his years—in fact, sometimes well beyond our understanding? We've said from the very beginning that we would place our trust in God in raising him. Maybe this is a reminder that we can trust God in what lies before us—and in what lies before Jesus. And maybe, just maybe, we're expecting too much of ourselves as well."

It was his turn for quiet. Slowly, he sat beside her and absorbed her words. "I know this, Joseph," continued Mary as she gently grasped his hands, her eyes softening as she looked into his. "You are the most kind and gentle man I know, and I thank God every day for the gift of your love. Somehow, together, we will find the best way to guide Jesus. God will see to it."

"Ah, Mary, my dear Mary," he sighed. "Yes, God has blessed us so and entrusted us with Jesus. You are right. When things stack up, and I get behind, I lose sight of that trust. I know God won't abandon us. Even so, may God give me patience as Jesus goes his own way."

He reached tenderly for her. They embraced, and Mary smiled.

*****

The early-morning solitude always brought inner peace and clarity for the day ahead. Ever since the boyhood episode in the temple, Jesus had come to cherish this time apart. The rabbis had called it *at one with the Holy*. After listening to the profound questions of the remarkable boy, they had encouraged him to adopt a spiritual regimen of solitude to grow deeper in that oneness. The practice puzzled his father, but with Mary's urging, Joseph had acquiesced and accepted it. "Just as long as he keeps up with his work," he had said. And he had to admit Jesus had never failed him.

Now Jesus sat upright and still, eyes closed. The day's communion with the Holy was complete, and his thoughts had returned to Moses and Elijah. There was much to glean from the experiences of the two sages.

The conversation with Moses hadn't taken him as far as he had hoped. Moses had endured consequences—grave consequences. So had Elijah. While the day alone with Moses had been entertaining and fascinating, the conversation too often had strayed. Surely the insight he was seeking—on staying true to purpose—rested within them. He must somehow take them deeper. Maybe with Elijah in the mix, he would be able to keep Moses focused. Jesus stood, stretched, and set out for the oasis.

*****

"I wasn't sure how long you would be, and Moses was getting hungry." Michael smiled, nodding toward Moses. "And you know how testy he can get. Won't you join us?" Moses ignored the slight, focusing instead on the meal spread before them. Elijah chuckled and waved his arm in greeting and invitation.

They were seated around a low stone with fresh bread, fruit, and cheese at its center. While still some distance away and drawn by the scent of the bread, the pup had abandoned Jesus and dashed ahead. Now as he approached, Jesus was suddenly hungry.

"That smells good." He smiled as he sat alongside and reached for the bread. "Still warm too!" He closed his eyes and savored a piece. "Mmm. I didn't realize I was hungry. Thank you, Michael. You are a blessing!"

"The food brings an added blessing, Jesus." Elijah grinned. "It keeps Moses quiet." Moses glared as he nibbled on a piece of cheese. Soon memories around bread and hunger brought lighthearted banter between the two, entertaining Jesus and Michael.

The meal finished, Jesus stood and walked to the water's edge. Dropping the tunic and kicking off his sandals, he dove into the pool with the pup at his heels. "A great start to the day!" he exclaimed. "Come on in!" Michael laughed, jumped up, and followed suit. Soon, all four were splashing each other as laughter filled the air. Even the pup had joined the fray.

*****

Refreshed from the dip in the pool, Jesus was seated with his back against the tree with the young jackal at his side, while Moses and Elijah were reclined on beds of leaves. Michael had wandered off.

Moses was regaling Elijah with stories of the exodus—of the forty years of the Hebrew people wandering in the desert after their escape from slavery in Egypt. Jesus sat enthralled as, with Elijah's prompting, the stories of the exodus unfolded. Of course, he was familiar with many of the stories from the reading of the ancient scrolls in the synagogue. But they came to life as Moses's eyes danced in the telling. Sadly, Jesus reflected, the stories recorded in the scrolls lacked Moses's humor in their telling. It pleased him that even when the journey was grim, Moses could relate moments of humor and laughter in the midst of the burdens.

"Keep in mind there were nearly two million of us wandering in the desert," Moses said in bringing his story to a close. "So when the quail came each evening[10]—enough meat to feed everyone—well, let's just say the quail left little reminders behind. And the next morning, sometimes those little "reminders" looked a lot like manna." He grinned. "So not all the manna tasted like honey, if you know what I mean."

The imagery caught Elijah and Jesus by surprise, and peals of laughter rolled across the desert floor. "You are sick," Elijah exclaimed, "very sick!" He turned to Jesus, who was trying to gather himself. "How long must I endure this?" he cried.

Moses sat in feigned innocence, proud of the effect of his story. Slowly, he stood and walked—more so, strutted—to the water's edge. He picked up a stone, tossed it into the pool, and watched the ripples fade as calm returned to Jesus and Elijah. He turned to them and shrugged. "I'm just saying, it wasn't always easy—even with all the miracles." He picked up another stone and tossed it into the pool. They all watched the ripples fade, an air of contemplation settling around them.

"You do have a way of telling stories with an entertaining twist, Moses." Jesus smiled. "Too bad the Scriptures don't reflect that." Moses grinned, and Elijah chuckled. Lighthearted banter had passed. Now Jesus turned solemn. "Moses, there is something I've been wondering about. I brought it up yesterday, but we didn't get very far." He turned to Elijah and explained, "We got sidetracked by more stories."

---

[10] Exodus 16:13

"Imagine that!" Elijah exclaimed, and laughed.

"Imagine, indeed." Jesus smiled. "But seriously, Elijah, your insight will be helpful too." He turned back to Moses. "You may remember it centers on *purpose*. So take us back to the early days of the exodus, Moses. As the people began to waver in following, how did you keep them in your heart even as they reviled you? Where did you find the strength to continue? They rejected you on so many occasions, and they rejected the God who had empowered you. How did you overcome the hurt, the pain, the anger which surely must have been within you?" Jesus was peering deeply into Moses's eyes. "How could you continue to reach out with compassion for them? And how did you find the strength to stay true to your purpose? How did you keep so firmly set on your purpose when the people you were called to lead and save rejected you so often?"

The change in Jesus's demeanor and the depth of his questions caught both Elijah and Moses by surprise. They sat silently for a few moments, absorbing all he had said.

In the midst of his confusion, Moses began. "This is odd, Jesus, the twist in this conversation. And as I said yesterday, it is odd engaging with you as the man Jesus, while knowing that you have all the power of the divine at your fingertips. Even more, you know what is to come—all that has been, which is, and which is to come. So this is just odd."

"Yes," Elijah interrupted. "We have watched you grow to manhood these thirty years, and you have experienced much good and some harm. Through it all, as a human, you have been blessed with two parents and the divine love they have received—all to prepare you for what lies ahead, the future which only you know."

"So it must be your human side which is asking these questions," Moses observed, "since your divine knows all. Is it your human side which wonders?"

Quiet settled over the threesome as Moses and Elijah intently studied his face. Slowly, Jesus leaned forward, picked up a pebble, and tossed it into the pond, his eyes fixed on the expanding ripples. Their eyes remained on him.

"Maybe so," Jesus acknowledged, still focused on the pond. "You are both here because I chose to become human, to live where humanity lives, to feel what humanity feels. Through the eyes of man, I have seen compassion and harm, hope and despair. More lies ahead in this journey. I have yet to experience all which life within time brings, but each of you have.

"I have observed many people waver from their convictions when things go wrong. And you are correct, Elijah. I have been fortunate because Mary and Joseph, the synagogue, indeed all of Nazareth, have helped shape my convictions while sheltering me from serious harm. However, all of that changed a few days ago with the baptism in the river. That moment set me on the path toward my purpose in entering time as a man.

"So, yes, I guess you're right." Jesus nodded, turning toward them. "The question before me is, as a man, will I be able to remain true to my purpose? Especially when I'm no longer under the shelter of home or village, of their support and encouragement. I must be *certain* I will remain true to my purpose regardless of what unfolds."

"Well then, Jesus," Elijah queried, "that begs the question: What *is* that purpose? Within the shackles of time, what do you hope to accomplish as a man that you couldn't accomplish as divine?"

The question startled Moses. Elijah had posed the question which had been eluding him. It was the same question, he suspected, which was at the root of Michael's confusion. It moved past the superficial *Why are we here?* to the essential: *Why has I AM entered time as a man—for what purpose?*

It hung in the air. Moses and Elijah waited expectantly, watching Jesus. Once again, he reached for a pebble, tossed it into the pond, and stared—deep in thought. Except for the ripples, all was still. When the last ripple reached the sand, Jesus turned to Elijah.

"These days in the wilderness are a part of that purpose," he said softly. "My coming encounters as a man with the satan are a part of that purpose. By the time I leave here, the purpose will be known"—he turned to Elijah with a smile—"but not today. Let's stretch our legs, before the heat of the noon sun is upon us. Come on, girl." He waved at the pup. "You look like you can use a break too." He jumped to his feet, picked a pear from the tree, and invited them with a wave. "I have more questions." He grinned.

*****

They delighted at the energy of the young pup as it danced in ever-widening circles around them. Tiring of the game, she turned to explore a small mound of rocks ahead. She yelped as a startled desert grouse erupted from its hiding place and flew low toward the horizon. The chase was on!

"We won't see her for the rest of the day," Jesus laughed. It was a leisurely stroll, each reflecting quietly on the earlier conversation. "I left home," Jesus continued, "telling Mary and Joseph it was time for me to live into the purpose before me. They have always encouraged me even when not understanding. As a father, I think Joseph was a little disappointed I was leaving the shop. Since I was the firstborn, he was hoping I would continue in the trade. He trusts me and my judgment as does Mary, but they don't understand. They will, but not today."

He turned silent, his gaze distant as though seeing beyond time.

"I know the heart of man, and I have watched men waver in their purpose. For my earthly purpose to unfold, I must remain steadfast. I know my human nature will be tested further and that whether through rejection or doubt, I must remain steadfast. Yes, Michael and all the heavenly beings protect and strengthen me in my humanity, but I alone bear the task of remaining steadfast to the purpose and bearing its consequence—I alone. And I must do that as a man.

He looked to Elijah. "You are correct: I know the divine intent, but I have watched some of the most stalwart fall short. You are both here, and especially you"—he turned to Moses—"because you know that enduring in the earthly realm can be very difficult. And that brings me to my greatest fear: How will my purpose be fulfilled if I can't endure?

He paused and then continued, "So Moses, what kept you steadfast to the purpose? Tell me how you endured when the people turned against you. What can I expect when I begin calling them back to life within the divine plan? Many have become settled in their ways—*stiff-necked*, I think you called them."

"Yes, stiff-necked," Moses reflected. "That is the effect of the satan, the ruler of the earthly realm. His power is always about, entering the lives of people when they least expect it, which is when they are the most vulnerable. Then comes the pain of rejection, the cursing, the spitting. You are correct"—he returned Jesus's gaze—"it was very difficult to endure." The memories were bringing back pain. He turned silent.

"And yet?" Jesus prompted.

"How did I?" Moses asked softly, turning to face him. "There is no mystery, Jesus. I could only endure by relying on I Am, the One who sent me, by putting all my trust there and the certainty that I Am was always available to me." He looked deep into Jesus's eyes. "After all, my purpose was not mine. My purpose belonged to I Am, not to me. It was always I Am working through me. I knew that. Maybe knowing that helped me remain true to I Am's purpose."

Their eyes were fixed on each other's. "Still it always perplexed me, Jesus," he continued, "and I think this speaks to the power of the satan's grip on humanity, that even with the mighty powers I Am worked through me, still the people were obstinate. Oh, they would turn to I Am for a time, but eventually, they'd fall away. That battle never seemed to end."

"I can vouch for that," Elijah chimed in. "Even by the time I came around many generations later, the people hadn't changed."

Slowly, Jesus turned and looked back toward the distant oasis, reflecting on the words of the two prophets. "That is why I have come into the earthly realm," he said, as though speaking to himself, "to live it firsthand, to experience the power and the grip of the satan, to truly *know* the circumstance in which *my* beloved live, to experience the pain and the depth of the separation when the gate to Eden was closed."[11]

They began retracing their steps in quiet.

---

[11] Genesis 3:23–24

"Has today been helpful, Jesus?" Moses asked.

"Yes," Jesus said, "very helpful. The answer I was seeking has come through you."

"And what was that?" Moses asked.

Jesus turned to him, a determined look in his eyes. "That *purpose* is of God, not of man—and that staying true to purpose rests in trusting that certainty."

DAY 7

Rest

On the seventh day, he rested.[12]

---

[12] Exodus 20:8–11

DAY 8

Morning
Preparing for the Satan

He was restless. Songbirds had awakened him in the predawn darkness. The symphony filled him, bringing back memories of early-morning childhood at home. Nazareth was quaint and intimate. Often he would quietly climb out of bed hours before dawn, his brothers deep in sleep. Then he would soak in the symphony of the birds, strolling slowly beneath the towering cypress.

Stretching, he reached for a nectarine. The fruit was cool from the crisp night air. It sharpened the flavor, evoking a smile as boyhood memories warmed him—memories of a time when heaviness belonged to others.

The soft rustle nearby of paws on the dusty soil interrupted the reverie. The jackal was softly padding to the pond's edge. With turned head, she studied Jesus, then slowly lowered her head to drink of the cool water. However, the quiet lapping did little to relax Jesus. The restlessness would not leave. As he pondered the day ahead, he shivered. It was not the crispness of the desert air. No—today, as Michael had arranged, he would meet the satan, his first one-on-one encounter with the fallen one. *Both in human form,* I Am had declared. This would be man to man.

It wasn't fear. No, it wasn't fear. The shiver ran through him as he contemplated the unknown, the uncertainty. *Storm,* as Michael had dubbed the satan from his encounter, was unpredictable. Through all of time, the nature of the satan when among the earthly beings was always unpredictable. And while the shape and behavior was always unpredictable, there was one constant—always, one constant: the relentless zeal to drive humanity from I Am.

Yet Michael had posed a different theory, one which was perhaps more plausible, even probable. Michael held that Storm's zeal was not driven by a desire to drive a wedge between humanity and I Am, nor to "win" people to his side in the cosmic struggle of good against evil or of darkness over light. No, Michael believed it was far more simple: that Storm's one desire—and one desire only—has been, is, and ever will be *to wound the heart of God.* The simplicity of Michael's theory had gripped him.

"Are you sure you will be okay?"

Deep in thought, the voice startled him. He turned. Michael was seated nearby, savoring a half-eaten apple and staring across the dark desert expanse toward the mauve horizon where the sun would soon greet the day.

"The satan can be very unpredictable, Jesus. You have seen people experience some of that during your years within time. Ask your parents. It was the satan who hardened the heart of King Herod, moving Herod to seek to destroy you as a baby by ordering the massacre of the children around Bethlehem. I Am intervened and sent the heavenly messenger to warn your father, leading Joseph and his family to flee to Egypt and avoid Herod's wrath.[13] So while, yes, I Am acted to keep you safe, the slaughter of the innocents left behind wounded the heart of the Eternal. We watched I Am grieve." Michael fell silent.

After a few moments, he turned to look at Jesus, then continued softly. "Are you sure you will be okay, alone?"

Jesus had been watching Michael intently while he spoke and had followed Michael's gaze to the unfolding sunrise. Now he could feel Michael's stare. "I'll be fine, Michael," he murmured. "The satan is curious. Storm, as you call him, will not harm me. The baptism at the river, the Spirit descending, and the voice—just as you have been

---

[13] Matthew 2:13–16

confused, so has Storm." Jesus turned to Michael with a wry smile. "Oh yes, there surely will be some surprises." He paused. "But Storm won't harm me. For now, curiosity has the better of him. I'll be fine." Jesus's gaze returned to the horizon, the sun poised to cast its first rays over the desert emptiness. "Beyond the far ridge, near the lone ancient oak? Did you agree on a time?"

"No, not a specific time," Michael replied. "I doubt time enters into Storm's thinking. I'm sure he'll be there when you arrive. Even though I didn't stick around for small talk, I'm sure you're right." He smirked. "Curiosity surely has the better of him!" They both chuckled. Michael watched the early-morning shadows slowly begin to recede across the emptiness. He was somber, his voice firm. "Even so, I don't trust him. I have never trusted him since he went his own way. And I would be failing you if I didn't speak of it. Just say the word, and I'll be alongside." Michael turned toward Jesus, determined. "I don't trust him, curiosity or not."

"Ah, Michael," Jesus said softly, his eyes glistening from Michael's underlying tenderness, "I'll be fine." After a few moments of silence, he continued, "This isn't the time for confrontation—Storm knows that." His focus was on the distant horizon. "I'll be fine."

*****

All was still, not a wisp through the leaves overhead, not a ripple disturbing the smooth surface of the spring-fed pool. Michael uneasily watched the distance grow between him and the lone figure as he neared the crest of the farthest ridge. Jesus had been firm, purposeful. He would meet Storm alone.

*****

He had waited until midmorning to avoid walking into the rising sun. His pace was steady though unhurried. In the desert, the distance to the horizon can be deceiving. The growing thirst reminded him of his humanness. Jesus smiled. Michael never argued, yet he could always depend on Michael to speak with conviction on matters which brought concern. The meeting with the satan had Michael on edge. "The satan can be very unpredictable, Jesus," he had warned.

Maybe so, Jesus thought, but he was grateful his earthly parents had prepared him well for encounters with the satan. Their confidence in I Am was unshakeable. They had instilled that same confidence in him from his earliest memories and surrounded him with faithful people who shared that confidence—who shared the certainty of the presence and power of I Am. Perhaps it is this human engagement with the satan which unsettles Michael so. It flows understandably from his protective nature, Jesus reflected. And while Jesus spoke confidently that he would withstand the wiles of the satan, it seemed Michael feared that the man, Jesus, was being naive. He chuckled softly. He was unconcerned about holding his own in a one-on-one. Yet if he were honest with himself, he confessed to a bit of trepidation in the unknown. It was trepidation which caused the early-morning shiver. Today he would experience firsthand as a man the nature of the satan in the earthly realm. Even so, he felt confident.

DAY 8

Midday
The Satan—Setting the Stage

The desert sun was nearly overhead as the ridge crest neared. The sand had warmed; soon his sandals would provide little comfort against the radiating heat. He turned and stared along the path he had come. The distant oasis was nearly indiscernible as a dark smudge on the vastness of the desert floor. The walk had taken longer than expected. He had declined Michael's offered water flask and was now beginning to regret it. Recalling Michael's description of the arid desolation where he had met Storm meant it would be a while before his thirst would be satisfied. At least he and the satan would be on equal footing.

He turned and continued walking toward the ridge. Fortunately, it would be downhill from there. Though still some distance from it, his eyes cleared the crest. He blinked and rubbed them. What seemed to stretch beyond the ridge confused him! Jesus broke into a trot, then a full run—and stopped breathless at the top, astonished!

A vast valley stretched below, twice as wide as the one left behind. Not far ahead down the slope, dry tufts of tinder grass added texture to the desert terrain. Further, a desert sage interrupted the thickening tinder until the dry grass gave way to an expanse of sage brush. A small herd of desert burros—playful foals frolicking about the jennies—grazed the tinder grass and sage. The lone jack, proud sentinel of his harem, raised his head and studied the intruder on the ridge. Sensing no threat, he lost interest and returned to his foraging. Beyond the sage, mesquites interrupted by an occasional scrub oak added more color and texture. At the center of the valley floor lay a vast carpet of lush greenery with palm, olive trees, and towering cedars, intersected by a meandering silver-blue thread. Animals of all kinds grazed in the verdant pastures along the gently flowing river, while birds soared lazily on the updrafts of the cloudless sky. Serenity filled the valley.

Nestled in the shade of a cedar grove on the far side of the river, a large cream-colored canopy stretched across a timber frame. Beneath the canopy, a figure arose, draped in a soft green robe, a gentle breeze playfully lifting its folds. With a wave of welcome, the figure beckoned him. Standing atop the ridge, Jesus returned the wave and absorbed the panorama stretching before him. *Unpredictable indeed*, he thought, recalling Michael's cautions. While he had no expectations around the encounter with the satan, this seemed out of character.

He started slowly down the ridge, eyes downcast to carefully navigate the stretch of rock-strewn desert. The fringe of tinder grass lay far ahead. It would take a while to reach the shade of the scrub oaks, let alone the cool waters of the meandering river. The overhead sun was relentless, without a hint of the breeze wafting across the distant valley floor.

Uneven footing made for slow progress down the gentle grade. Soon he looked back to see how far he had come from the ridgetop and was dismayed. At this rate, it would be late afternoon before reaching the cool stream, and the cloudless sky would bring no relief from the sun. Wiping the sweat from his brow, he turned and continued slowly, intensely focused on the rocky terrain. The sound of a shuffle lifted his eyes. He paused. Not far ahead, a lone burro had come to a halt and was eyeing him warily. The colt looked back to those far behind, then continued slowly toward Jesus. It picked its footing carefully in the uneven ground as the distance separating them slowly diminished.

Soon it stood at arm's length, ears alert, dark-gray eyes nervously focused on him. Light-colored forelegs darkened into uppers.

The neck and back of a rich brown blended down the sides to a cream-colored underbelly. Dark brown ears were fringed in black, complementing the black mane and tail. It was clearly the offspring of the sentinel. Curiosity had instilled the jack's confidence, but skittish eyes betrayed the youth of a colt. Jesus smiled and slowly extended his right hand. The colt cautiously stretched its neck until Jesus could feel the moist warmth from the twitching nostrils of the soft dark nose. He stood motionless while the jittery colt satisfied its fears. Slowly, the gray tongue explored a fingertip, then the fingers, until it found the back of his hand which still bore the sweat from his forehead. The colt found delight in its saltiness.

Jesus noticed something peculiar. With fear subsided, the colt was nuzzling him in search of more. Straddling its shoulders was a vine the length of a man's arm and, tied to either end, a yellow gourd with a bulb the size of a melon. Each gourd was corked at the tip of its stem. With the colt busy licking his sandals, Jesus cautiously lifted the vine and the gourds and draped them around his neck. Slowly, he uncorked one and guardedly sniffed its contents. Nothing. With his left hand, he tilted it to the side, his open right hand against the spout. The clear liquid was cool to his palm. Again he sniffed; it was odorless. Warily, he tasted the liquid in his palm—and smiled. The gourds were filled with cool water!

He turned to the far canopy; the standing figure was watching. Jesus smiled and waved. The distant figure waved in reply.

He raised the first gourd to his lips and savored the moment as the cool, clear water brought instant relief. Emptying the first one fully refreshed, he raised the second and slowly poured cool water over his head and brow. The distant figure waved again, beckoning him. Jesus nodded and turned to the colt. Pouring the last of the water into his cupped hand, he held it until the colt was satisfied. Slowly taking hold of the mane, Jesus straddled the colt gingerly. The colt's skittishness had disappeared. The ride to the valley floor and to the welcoming stranger would pass quickly.

Even under heavy load, the colt was surefooted down the rocky terrain. Reaching the tinder grass, it trotted confidently and slowed to a walk as the small herd neared. They parted as the colt approached, staring inquisitively at the strange rider. Once past the herd, the ground flattened, and the colt's gait quickened. It seemed drawn to the canopy and the figure in its shade. Jesus's gaze was drawn to the figure as well. They were approaching the river. On the far shore, a long stone's throw across, the gently billowing canopy nestled in the shade of the rustling cedars. With the rippling current in the foreground, the setting was serene and inviting.

The figure was standing under the canopy watching, yet the distance was too great to make out distinguishing features. He was loosely draped in the soft green robe of lightweight material. A similar material in pale blue formed a loose-fitting headdress, while a matching blue sash gathered the robe loosely around the waist. He was barefoot.

The colt slowed, uncertain how to navigate the flowing water and deliver its passenger to the other side. It stopped at the foot of the pebble-covered bank, lifted its head, and brayed. Jesus laughed and stepped onto the shore. Now suddenly free, the colt bolted and ran a short distance, stopped, and brayed again. Then it turned, broke into a nervous gallop, and retraced its steps toward the distant herd. Jesus's eyes followed the colt for a moment, then turned to the cloaked figure on the other side whose eyes were on him. The murmur of the river current and the breeze in the trees muffled the call, but he caught just enough, "Swim across...halfway..."

Remembering the journey before the colt surprise, he looked down at the dust-encrusted sandals. A dip in cool water would be refreshing indeed! Stripping his tunic and loincloth, he gathered them above his head with one hand to reserve the other for a swimming stroke. To his surprise, the cloaked figure had removed the headdress. When the waist sash fell, the robe slipped off her shoulders. In the sunlight, her bronze beauty dazzled. With three quick strides to the water's edge, she dove and began stroking toward him. He was dumbfounded, eyes bulging and mouth agape, momentarily transfixed!

After several strokes, she stopped, stood erect in the waist-deep water, her deep-brown eyes fixed alluringly on him. Sensuous lips parted in a mischievous smile, pleased with her surprise. She flicked her head playfully from side to side, the long dark tresses falling short of the water as they cascaded across her breasts. They were full, perfectly proportioned.

"Are you coming, or have you had enough?" she taunted. "I said I'd meet you halfway. Come on, do your part!" He blinked, catching his breath.

"Be right there," he shouted, dropping his wrap and kicking off the sandals. "I'll be halfway before you can call out your name!"

The chill of the water only heightened his excitement as he boldly stroked toward her, pulling up just short. She hadn't moved. He was breathing heavily, no doubt from the strong current and the rush to prevail in the race to halfway. *But no*, he confessed silently, *it was the excitement of being caught short by her abrupt nakedness.* He rose from the water and stood before her, entranced. Never had Jesus seen such stunning beauty!

She was a half hand shorter, exquisite in every detail. Against a warm bronze face, her brown eyes danced—a teasing dance—her lips and smile, inviting. Casually, she reached for his hands and slowly traced her fingers along his muscular arms until they rested on broad shoulders. Her eyes were fixed on his, but his were drawn to the rest of her. In the swirling clear water, her hips danced; her breasts swayed.

His eyes returned to hers. "I thought you said halfway," he said in a playful, yet accusatory tone.

"I lied," she teased, breathing into his ear, her breasts brushing lightly against his chest. "And besides," she demurred, tracing her upper lip with her tongue, "you kept me waiting." With a casual nod, she retraced his arm, took one hand in hers, and started to wade back to shore. When he tugged lightly, she turned in profile. "What?" she asked, searching his eyes.

"You didn't call out your name." He smiled. "I said I'd meet you halfway before you could call out your name. You didn't call out your name."

The alluring smile returned. She tossed her head, dark hair taunting. "You can call me *Delilah*," she replied, her eyes dancing.

"Delilah," he mused guardedly, reflecting on the Philistine woman whose treachery and wiles had led to the demise of mighty Samson.[14]

The afternoon unfolded with delight following delight. Turning toward shore, Delilah slid to his right side and gently pulled his arm around her lower back, cupping his hand lightly on her hip, her hand resting on his to gently hold it in place. Her left arm draped across his lower back, her hand on his hip. The flowing water was cool and refreshing. As one, they turned to face the meandering current and slowly—ever so slowly—began wading into it. With the warm breeze in his face, the serene beauty of sun-dappled trees lining the banks, and the feel of her alongside as the water playfully swirled around them, Jesus's thoughts wandered in reverie—the allure of her smile, the eyes which enchanted, the tease of her nature and, above all, the stunning beauty. What would be the harm of an afternoon of pleasure? There would be time for purpose later. For now, what would be the harm in pleasure?

He glanced toward her. Her gaze was fixed on the leaves shimmering in the gentle breeze. Almost as though reading his mind, Delilah gently slid his hand from her hip, wrapped his arm further around, and softly cupped his hand under her breast. She continued to study the leaves. His gaze absently followed hers, but his thoughts followed his hand. The water swirled as they continued the slow walk, enjoying all about them.

Delilah paused and turned her head toward him, her hand continuing to hold his at her breast. "You must be hungry." She smiled softly. "When did you eat last?"

His free hand rose to hold her face. "I wasn't thinking of food." He smiled. "But now that you mention it, I *am* hungry. This morning's fruit was a while ago."

"Well, I've prepared something for us to nibble on." She smiled, turning to face him. Her hands rose to his shoulders, her breasts lightly against him. "Why don't we head back, get comfortable, and

---

[14] Judges 16:4–21

see what satisfies? I think you'll like it"—her eyes danced—"since you're hungry."

She laid her head on his shoulder as he pulled her close. The scent of her hair was otherworldly, feeding his senses. As her hands slipped slowly to his hips, he could feel the excitement grow.

*****

"Something's bothering you, Michael," Elijah said as their stroll brought them back to the cool water in the shade of the tree. The late-day sun was at their back, dusk not far off. "You've been a little tense for most of the afternoon. Everything all right?"

Michael's eyes were searching. "He's not here," he sighed. "He should be back by now. It will soon be dark." He was agitated, trying hard to control it. "I knew I should have gone with him." They had reached the tree, Michael now pacing back and forth. "Jesus has not had to deal with Storm as a human. A man is no match for the wiles of the satan." He breathed deeply. "I should have gone with him. He didn't want me to, but I've had to deal with Storm too many times." He turned to Elijah. "Maybe we should go find them. If we hurry, we could get there before it gets too dark."

Elijah gathered a handful of leaves, dusted off a stone next to the pool, and sat. "Maybe you can go, Michael, but we've been walking most of the afternoon, and I'm beat." He shook off the sandals and swirled his feet in the cool water. "I'm done for the day. If you feel you must, go ahead."

Michael pivoted and glared at Elijah. "I have one purpose and one purpose only, Elijah," he exclaimed. "To serve I Am completely. Here within the constraint of time, that purpose is the same—to be alongside I Am as the man, Jesus, without reservation. No excuses." His eyes were fixed on the horizon where Jesus had disappeared. "Something is wrong. I can just feel something is wrong."

"Didn't he tell you to stay?" Elijah asked. "Isn't that what you said this morning?"

"Yes," Michael snapped, "that was his instruction, even though he knew I didn't like it. He said there was nothing to fear because he believed their time together would be more about satisfying the satan's curiosity. He was confident of being able to stand his own. In fact, he told me not to worry!"

Elijah stretched out on the bed of leaves. "Well, Michael," he sighed, "that's good enough for me. Why not rest for a bit? We're both tired, and that old tree is a lot further than you think. Lighten up and quit worrying." He looked at Michael. "I've got a feeling Jesus knows what he's doing, and he'll have the upper hand." He sighed and rolled over. "What's the old saying? *There's always tomorrow.* So give it a rest!"

DAY 8

Evening
The Satan—Lust

Jesus breathed a quiet sigh of contentment. The light fabric of the cream-colored canopy provided soft shade and spacious shelter, though none was needed from the warm, gentle breeze. Across the shelter floor stretched an array of soft lambs' wool carpet, woven in complementary brilliant and subdued hues. Vases of calla lilies tastefully adorned the space; a subtle incense filled the air.

Near the rear lay a luxurious sleeping mat for two, sheathed in cool blue silk with sensuous matching pillows at head and foot. Under the canopy center, large pillows of finest Egyptian cotton formed an inviting area for intimate conversation. Reclining pillows surrounded the low table nearby where finger bowls and serving platters heaped with nectarines, grapes, and dates waited. Two royal-blue porcelain chalices nestled against plump wineskins. At the far corner just beyond the canopy, a fire pit was lined with smooth river rock. Glowing embers from a midday cooking fire warmed the two spit-roasted desert grouse. A fresh loaf of bread rested on the flat baking stone nearby. The aromas of lily and incense, freshly baked bread, and roasted grouse reminded him of his hunger. But it was her scent—a subtle and mysterious scent—which held him. It wasn't hunger which gripped him. It was enchantment—a feeling new to him.

Delilah had retrieved the soft green silken robe and draped it casually from her shoulders, gathering it loosely at the waist with the periwinkle sash. The folds fell gently, yet nothing was concealed. His eyes followed her every movement.

"Here." She smiled, leaning close and handing him a matching robe. "Maybe the cool stream still has you in its spell. You seem to be at a loss for words." The folds opened as her breasts fell free. Her eyes were inviting. "Or is there something else?" she demurred, slowly sinking onto the conversation pillows. The sash had fallen free, leaving the robe unfettered. As she reclined against the pillows, the robe slipped to reveal her shoulder. With a free hand, she gathered her long dark hair and draped it loosely over the shoulder. She was now fully reclined on her side, the silk robe of little effect, her head propped by the other arm for intimacy. Delilah's eyes had not left his. "Is something on your mind?" she purred, patting the pillow alongside her. "There's no rush, is there? Let's let the night unfold." She motioned him to join her.

He took the robe and laid it casually on the mat, then lowered himself to lie facing her. She studied his face, while he studied all of her. In the early-evening light, with candles and incense in the air, he was entranced. Her beauty, her loveliness, was like none other. The bronze tone of her skin was unchanging the length of her body, accented by the dark flowing hair and by the dark crop at the joining of her thighs. His gaze returned to hers. Her lips parted as she slowly moistened them. She reached for his hand and drew it near her—first to her breast, and then slowly lower.

Jesus closed his eyes as her hand caressed his chest, then slowly moved downward. With closed eyes too, she caressed his intimacy. The exploring, the caressing was unhurried, each enjoying the growing pleasure of gentle intimacies. As daylight faded to twilight, the murmur of sounds of the unfolding evening blended with the intimacy in the air.

*****

The meal had been delicious, and the wine like none he could recall—the bread, the roasted grouse, the fruit, all perfectly capped with the wine. They were reclined alongside the table—chalices within casual reach—he on his back, she nestled beside him. Soft laughter had framed the pleasure of feeding each other, with moments of playfulness as dates and grapes eluded their intended targets. The dying embers transformed the canopy ceiling into a soft glow as moonlight danced beyond its reach.

Slowly so as not to disturb her, Jesus reached for the chalice. She turned and smiled. "Just what I was thinking," she said softly. He placed it to her lips, and she sipped slowly. "Very nice, if I do say so myself. Very nice."

"Yes," he said, bringing it to his lips, "very nice indeed." He drank slowly, emptying it. "You have brought pleasure at a most unexpected time, in a most unexpected place." He had never felt so satisfied.

"Well," Delilah whispered softly and glanced toward the sleep mats, "the evening awaits."

Jesus reached for the wineskin, refilled the chalice, and chuckled. *"There's no rush, is there? Let's let the night unfold.* Seems like I've heard that before," he chided. Delilah giggled softly and snuggled closer. "But before sleep comes, we must explore why Michael arranged for this day. And the setting"—he cast his eyes beyond the canopy into the moonlit night, glistening on the meandering stream—"is not what he had described. And this certainly is not what I was expecting."

"Oh, good. I've surprised you then." She smiled. "You're not disappointed, are you?" She pouted and teasingly stroked her hair. "Every man desires a little pleasure now and then. That's been true since the very beginning. So I thought it would be fun to meet someplace and in a way you've not experienced." She paused, her eyes dancing as she peered into his. "Have I disappointed you?"

"Disappointed me?" Jesus smiled. "Oh my, no. Surprised me, yes. But not disappointed. Perhaps unknowingly, you have given me the gift of experiencing desire as it enters the heart of man. Having experienced it will help me in what is to come." He turned thoughtful and reached for a fig, followed by a sip of wine, then paused and studied the chalice against the moonlight. "This wine is delightful, and mysterious—almost as though desire flows from it."

"Good." She smiled, slowly tracing her fingers along his arm. "I thought it would please you."

But curiosity was getting the better of Delilah. She sat up. "We haven't had a chance to really get to know each other since you entered time. I have been watching very closely these thirty years. All along I confess that you have me wondering—wondering why you have come into the earthly domain, into *my* domain." In an instant, her eyes hardened, and her demeanor changed. "Michael, that doddering messenger, was useless," she snapped. "He doesn't have a clue." Her tone was biting, derisive as she recalled the meeting a week ago with Michael in the desert emptiness.

Before he could react, Delilah caught herself. Just as quickly, the hardness disappeared. Her eyes softened; her lips parted. "You are so strong, Jesus, and so gentle," she purred, regaining her self-control. She reclined, her fingers softly tracing along his side, then pausing at his hip. "In time, you will share your thinking," she whispered with a quiet confidence as she drew close, her fingers continuing slowly downward.

He brought his hand gently to hers, stopping it short. "Ah, Delilah, you are a tease." He smiled, holding her eyes with his. "A delightful tease, to be sure—and a very confident one!" He chuckled, turning his eyes to her hand in his. "But for a moment there," he continued slowly, "your curiosity took over, and just a hint of temper showed. Michael warned me about that temper and how quickly it can turn." His eyes returned to hers. "What is it between you and Michael that sets you off so?"

Delilah's eyes were soft and inviting. She lowered herself to fully recline, the soft cushions against her back. Slowly, she drew his hand to her breast and, with the other, pulled him close. "Tonight is for you and me, Jesus, "she purred, "just you and me."

Somewhere in the gentle breeze, the murmuring stream, the incense, the wine, her scent—somewhere, somehow his thoughts left him as his defenses weakened.

DAY 9

Michael
Rescue

When Jesus had not returned by sundown, Michael's thoughts ran wild. Jesus had insisted on going alone, and his words had been clear: "I'll be fine," he had said. "This isn't the time for confrontation—Storm knows that. I'll be fine." Elijah had fallen into a deep sleep and was of no help.

Michael wasn't so sure. The night had been long and fitful, and now dawn was near with no sign of Jesus. His instincts were working against him, and his lack of understanding only heightened his concerns. Could the man Jesus have underestimated the satan? Or could the man Jesus have been overconfident of his own abilities? Confusion or not, he could wait no longer. Elijah hadn't moved; there was no reason to wake him.

Not knowing what might lay ahead, Michael knelt at the edge of the spring and drank deeply—again and again. After picking a few pieces of fruit and donning the cloak to protect against the sun, he set out at a brisk pace across the desert expanse toward the distant horizon, carefully following Jesus's tracks. In a few minutes, the rising sun would be directly in his eyes. At this pace, he was confident of reaching the crest of the distant horizon by midmorn. The determination in his stare was matched by his stride. He recalled that days earlier once past the crest, the downward slope had made the heat less oppressive. He had no idea then how the day would unfold, and at this moment, he felt the same way.

The gradual but steady incline and the relentless heat from the sun as it inched toward midday was having an effect. It had been further than he expected to the ridge, and the determination in his stride had lessened. As it neared, his pace quickened. He paused at the crest, catching his breath. Everything looked as before: the vast expanse of desert emptiness stretching far into the distance, interrupted by the tiny forlorn skeleton of the ancient oak which had endured Storm's onslaught. But no Jesus. He had been sure that when he reached the crest, he would find Jesus walking toward him—and together they would return to the shaded oasis with its spring-fed pool.

Shifting his gaze to the slope before him, Jesus's footprints continued in the direction of the petrified tree. The gentle downward slope would be effortless compared to the past few hours. With no sign of Jesus, concern creased his face, and determination returned. Any thought of thirst or weariness was swept away. He had failed in being alongside. *I should have trusted my instincts*, he thought, one foot ahead of the other at a measured, rapid clip. *I've dealt with the satan, and Jesus hasn't. I should not have let him go alone.*

Suddenly, his thoughts were erased by a more urgent reality. The footprints had disappeared…gone! He stopped, fearfully scanning the ground before him. Nothing. He quickly raised his head and stared into the distance. The desert sand stretched uninterrupted as far as he could see, well beyond the distant skeleton. Quickly, he twirled around and studied the path left by his footprints. Alongside them, a second set of prints—the ones he had been following!

Michael turned to the distant tree, cupped his hands to his mouth and bellowed, "*Jesus!*" His cry echoed into the distance. "Jesus," he yelled. "Jesus!" No reply. Nothing. Only stillness in the desert heat. *Oh dear God*, Michael cried.

He has to be at the tree, he thought. *That's where they were to meet. Where else could he be—and what has happened to him?* No longer thinking about the relentless sun or thirst or weariness, he threw off the cloak and broke into a fast trot, eyes focused on the distant skeleton. Surely a clue lay somewhere there.

He ran swiftly, relentlessly, but his humanity was bogging him down. His bronze skin burned beneath the sun. Sweat rolled from every pore, his body glistening. The sweat from his brow stung his eyes, but nothing could slow him. *Is the satan behind this devilish sun and the scorching sand?* his mind raced. *Was this Storm getting even?* No matter. Nothing could stop him. His focus was finding Jesus.

Slowly, very slowly, the gnarled skeleton was becoming more discernable. A week ago, he had studied it intently and wondered of the testimony it could give. Surely nothing through the dormant centuries could compare to whatever yesterday brought. Michael's eyes had been focused on the tree from the moment the footprints had disappeared. He stopped for a moment, pausing to wipe the sweat from his forehead and clear his gaze.

Then he saw it. A short distance from the tree, it lay motionless on the ground. A low-profile rock? A lone desert shrub? He stared, but the distance hid any clue. "Jesus!" he yelled. Only quiet across the desert emptiness. During his earlier visit, there had been nothing to interrupt the desert sand but the twisted skeleton. Of that he was certain. *Something* had changed since he had delivered I Am's message. "Jesus!" he yelled again. Nothing.

He was racing toward the empty tree, eyes fixed on the mystery. No, as he neared, it wasn't a rock—and if a shrub, it was oddly out of place. Surely he would have noticed it before. "Jesus!" he yelled again, nearly breathless from running. And still nothing. He stopped, soaked in perspiration and gasping for air, now just fifty paces away. His stare was unwavering, fixed on the motionless mass, the gasps turning into deep, measured breaths. Slowly he stepped forward, fixated on the elongated shape.

It was a body! As he neared, it appeared to be wrapped in a shroud of light green. The feet were exposed; the head covered with a soft blue wrap. It was lying on a cream-colored mat, its head resting on a royal-blue silken pillow. As Michael drew near, something stirred—and suddenly, the head of the young jackal appeared above the chest. The pup stood and stretched, tail wagging and eyes focused on Michael. She let out an excited yip, then nestled her nose against the neck of the still body, growling playfully, but the body remained motionless.

Michael approached slowly, quietly. Were these burial wraps? And how had the body gotten here? The pup was now at the feet of the body, slowly licking them while Michael watched in confusion. His gaze turned from the pup and looked closely at the body wrap. Wait! There was slow, measured motion in the chest. It was breathing! Gingerly, he reached for the head linen and pulled it aside.

Jesus was fast asleep.

DAY 10

Jesus and Michael
Subtlety

The leaves overhead rustled in the soft breeze as the symphony of birds reached their crescendo. Soon the stars would fade as dawn neared. The pup's lapping at the pool's edge had awakened him. He lay quietly, staring into the leaf-laden branches, listening to the sounds of the night. Sleep on the bed of leaves had been deep and peaceful, a welcome relief from the confusion and stress of yesterday. Turning his head, he could make out the shape of Jesus lying nearby and faintly hear the slow, rhythmic breathing of a man deep in sleep. The pup had returned to its bed at Jesus's side.

Michael's thoughts turned to the day before. Upon discovering that Jesus was safe, he had settled nearby in the shadow of the ancient trunk and rested against it—and waited. His presence had excited the pup, and soon it was licking Jesus's face. Jesus had slowly opened his eyes to find the nose of the quivering pup a whisker from his and chuckled. The pup had jumped in surprise, causing both Michael and Jesus to laugh.

Michael had shared his story of concern and relief in finding him safe and then peppered him with questions about the disappearing footprints in the sand, his meeting with Storm, and the peculiar bedding. Jesus had smiled but remained tight-lipped. "You and I were both right," he had said. "Let's just say our time together was framed in mutual curiosity." Then he had reached for a yellow gourd alongside him—corked at its tip—and handed it to Michael. The water had been cool and refreshing.

Donning his tunic and sandals, Jesus and Michael set out across the desert floor toward their oasis home. "What about the bedding and water gourd?" Michael asked. They turned and looked back. The petrified tree was standing alone and forlorn in the surrounding emptiness with no evidence of any human visitation. No sleeping mat, no pillow, no shroud. Jesus smiled—and remained silent about the encounter with Storm. *Maybe today,* Michael thought. *Surely I'll learn more today.* Today, there would be answers. After Jesus awoke, he would get to the bottom of the visit with Storm. Still exhausted, Michael rolled over and fell asleep.

*****

"Well, Michael"—Jesus smiled—"the last couple of days must have taken a toll. You've missed a beautiful morning!" It was midday, and Jesus was leaning against the trunk and enjoying a nectarine. "You must be hungry, so help yourself. I hope you enjoy it." Jesus had arranged a bed of leaves at the pool's edge. It was the aroma of fresh bread and grilled fish over the cooking fire that had invaded Michael's sleep.

Michael sat up, stretched his arms toward his feet, and yawned. "Being human and within time is always an adjustment, Jesus. And sleep—especially a deep sleep—is like being free of time and free of aches and stiffness. And then abruptly, sleep gives way to time and the realities of yesterdays." He looked around. "You're right. I didn't realize I was hungry. Oh boy, fresh bread and fish!" He leaped up, crossed quickly, and knelt beside the pool and drank deeply of the cool water. "Are you going to join me?" he asked as he reclined on the leaves and reached for the bread. "Or have you already eaten?"

"I was waiting for you." Jesus laughed and tossed him a fig. "But if you hadn't woken up pretty soon, you were going to be eating alone." He settled on the leaves and nibbled on a piece of fish. "There is something about fish and the sea," he mused. "I'm drawn to them—to fish and the sea. Maybe it's because Nazareth was so far from the sea, and when we went as a family, it was always special. And the fishermen with their boats and nets, it just always seemed their livelihood was not their own, that they knew that whatever plenty they enjoyed was a gift and not of their doing. I find myself drawn to them." His eyes were distant as he recalled those rare childhood visits to Galilee and watching the fishermen along the shore. "However things unfold during the days ahead, it wouldn't surprise me that there will be some time along the sea in whatever is to come."

Michael sat pensively, absently enjoying the bread and fish. So many questions were flying through his mind he could hardly control himself: What had happened in the past two days? What had Jesus learned about Storm, and what had Storm learned about him? Why had Jesus wanted to meet with Storm anyway? And what is this time in the wilderness all about? And the deeper question which hasn't left him: why has I Am chosen to step into humanity and the shackles of time? What is going on? It had been more than a week, and things seemed even more confusing.

The barrenness of the sprawling desert wilderness was deceiving. As the days had slowly unfolded, all manner of wild creatures were drawn to the shade canopy and spring-fed pool. Skittish at first, the animals had learned there was nothing to fear from the two-footed strangers who had come into their world. The confident man in particular seemed to find delight in each creature. Clearly the jackal pup had found delight in him as well and was never far from his side.

Now whatever pressures Jesus had been feeling ebbed as he watched creatures at play and called them by name. For an hour or more, lighthearted laughter filled the air, but he sensed Michael's uneasiness. Eyes fixed on the life around him, Jesus rose slowly to his feet. With a slow wave of his hand, the creatures began to drift away until all was quiet. He turned to Michael. "Feel like taking a walk?" he asked. "Stretch our legs a bit before the heat gets unbearable?"

"Sounds like a good idea." Michael came alongside, his eyes on the distant ridge. "Any place in particular? Did you leave something behind?" he asked with a suggestive lilt.

Jesus chuckled. "Cute, Michael, that's cute." A smile creased his face.

Michael turned, saw the smile and laughed. "Well, it's been ten days, and I'm more confused than when we began. I kind of thought that when you met Storm, some answers would come." His gaze returned to the horizon. He continued slowly, "Yet you've been quiet. Something is going on, and you've been quiet."

The falcon had returned and found Jesus's shoulder, the pup not far behind. Jesus reached down and patted the pup's head, and it fell alongside.

"It's the humanity, Michael, that has brought surprises," Jesus began, "and the surprises the satan tossed my way. I admit to being quiet since the time with Storm. The entire experience was...unexpected. As a man, I had hoped to learn firsthand the ways of Storm. And from the moment I reached the ridge on the way to the ancient tree, surprise after surprise unfolded. I was confident of being alert and in full control.

"Yet the biggest surprise and what has me so perplexed is how subtle is the effect of the satan to sway a man's confidence—and how the man doesn't even realize he is being swayed. Innocent moments of delight slowly lead to more and more innocent moments, until all of a sudden, you realize that the path you're on has taken you away from your core convictions. Worse, a man can begin to think those convictions have been wrong all along as he experiences a new way of looking at things. The logic that has served him so well gets muddled as convictions begin to weaken. Reflecting on the experience from this side of it, I can now see how my feelings, my emotions, were being affected. So subtle and so powerful are the ways that twist the desire for intimate pleasure and then lead to harm."

Their pace had slowed and now came to a stop. Jesus gazed across the creatures scattered near and far, some at rest, some grazing on the meager scrub, and some at play. The falcon darted away, soaring in wide loops. Jesus smiled and watched quietly. At peace, he turned and slowly began retracing their steps toward the cool of the distant oasis. Seeing a shift in direction, the falcon returned to the shoulder roost.

Jesus fell silent. The time with Delilah had unsettled him. It was, in fact, *he* who had sent Michael to tell the satan to meet him at the old oak. He had intended to demonstrate firsthand—and prove both to the satan and to himself—that as a man, he could prevail over anything the satan might throw at him. Yet through the allure of Delilah, he had to admit that the satan had rattled him—that Jesus had allowed himself to postpone the purpose he had in mind. *After all,* he recalled thinking with Delilah at his side, *what would be the harm of an afternoon of pleasure? There would be time for purpose later.* In convincing himself that his purpose for the visit could be postponed he had, in fact, failed. He had failed to stay true to his purpose, and worse, the satan had swayed him without much of a fight! If desire and lust could divert him from the singular purpose of this introductory visit, what might unfold in matters of graver consequence? The conversation with Moses and Elijah about staying true to purpose had taken on far greater significance.

"Storm doesn't realize it," he shared, "but our time together was a huge gift for what lies ahead. To expect the unexpected. Be vigilant. Trust your convictions to know when to stand firm or when to turn away. Above all, trust the source of your convictions, the source of your purpose."

Michael listened attentively. Jesus had shared very little of the detail around his time with Storm, and that only added to his confusion. Jesus was describing some of the ways of the satan, but those ways were not new to Michael or to any of the heavenly beings. Surely none of this could be new to Jesus.

Before he could speak, Jesus turned to him. "I know your thoughts, Michael," he said. "Yes, you have watched the ways of the satan through all of time, and yes, none of this is new." Michael's eyes were fixed on him. Jesus breathed deeply, then sighed. "But *feeling* it, *living* it as a human—*experiencing* the nature of the satan firsthand— to feel the grip held over the human heart since time came into the earthly realm, I want to *know* that grip, to *feel* that grip, to *confront* that grip. These couple of days have been part of that. Still more lies ahead." He breathed slowly, and his eyes hardened with conviction. "More lies ahead. But for now, some time for solitude and fasting is before me."

"How long will it take?" Michael asked. "How long will we be in this human form, and how long here in this place? What is your plan?"

Jesus smiled and turned on the path toward the cool spring water, picking up the pace. "A plan?" He chuckled. "A plan? You sound like Joseph when I left home a few months ago, 'Where are you going, and what are you going to do? What is your plan?'" His chuckle grew into a full throated laugh. "If only he could see me now! He would be more confused than you!"

Michael joined in the laughter. The pup skittered away from them in surprise which caused the falcon to leap from Jesus's shoulder. The two jousted back and forth in their game as they headed playfully toward the oasis. Laughter echoed across the desert floor. Soon they arrived.

"Please tell Elijah I wish to devote time with him in a few days, maybe in a week or two. After my solitary fast, I will spend a little more time with Moses, so ask him to return. And then, I'd like to visit with David, son of Jesse. Would you arrange that please?"

"King David?" Michael asked, a look of bewilderment on his face.

"David, son of Jesse…father of Solomon. Yes, King David."

DAYS 11,12

Jesus
Solitude and Fasting

Once again, Jesus left before dawn for the distant outcropping, carrying only a flask of water.

That purpose is of God, not of man, he had replied to Moses, *and staying true to purpose rests in trusting that certainty.* Yet the satan had caused him to face squarely the human capacity to remain true to purpose.

In the days and weeks ahead, how to remain steadfast in purpose?

DAY 13

Moses
Doubt

"But after all the power I Am had delivered through you to save them, the people still doubted." Jesus's eyes had narrowed, and his tone hardened. "And at Meribah, even you doubted.[15] Why? Why did *you*—of all people and after all you had witnessed and experienced—why did *you* doubt the power of I Am in that moment?"

At first, the give and take had been fun, and he was glad they were alone, but now the questions were becoming annoying. Moses was losing his patience. The more Jesus probed, he realized, the more discomfort he felt. *Why am I still here,* he wondered, *and what is he seeking now?* He stared at Jesus, silently wishing Elijah hadn't left.

"You know, Jesus," he replied testily, "you're bringing up an old wound, a wound I had long ago put behind me. Yes, you're correct. For one brief moment facing that boulder at Meribah—when all the anger and doubts of the people were directed at me—in that moment, *I* doubted whether water could flow from a worthless rock in the middle of that God-forsaken wasteland. So when I struck it with my staff, and nothing happened, my anger took over, and I hit it again. And yes, the water flowed—and because of that *one* moment of doubt and anger, I paid a heavy price." Moses was defiant, the earlier lightheartedness gone.

---

[15] Numbers 20:12

Jesus sat quietly for a few moments watching Moses and then continued, "Yes, you did"—his eyes softening—"you and all those who doubted." The story of an unfaithful generation deprived of entering the Promised Land had been recounted in homes and synagogues by generations ever since—as had the telling of the continuing mercy and faithfulness of I Am toward those who entered and remained faithful. "Even so, you haven't answered my question."

Moses' face hardened, and his glare intensified. Though he could see the softening in Jesus's eyes, he struggled to keep control as anger rose inside. Jesus was probing at the place of his deepest hurt, and he didn't like it. "Why are we coming back to this?" he snapped. "What more do you want from me? Why did you have me brought back here, as a man, back into time? For this? To make me relive the moment of my deepest despair when I Am declared I would not enter the Land of Promise after everything I had done? Over that one moment of doubt?

"I didn't understand then, and I died with a broken heart. I thought all of that was in the past, buried when I died. So you have Michael bring me back—for what? Why am I still here? Are you taking pleasure in watching me relive that deep pain?" The furrowed brow and narrowed eyes were the best he could do to contain the hurt. Slowly, with rising intensity and trembling voice, Moses implored, "What more do you want from me?" Anguish overcame him. Eyes brimming with tears, he crumpled to his knees, lowered his head, and sobbed.

Jesus watched in surprise at the unexpected transformation from the brash and braggart Moses to the man crumpled before him. Sorrow filled him as he realized the pain his question had caused.

"Oh, Moses," he said softly, placing his hand on the bowed head. His voice wavered. "I am so sorry you are in such deep pain and regret my questions have brought it to you. I am so sorry. Can you forgive me for reviving that pain?"

Slowly, Moses lifted his head. To his surprise, the tears in Jesus's eyes matched his own. As he struggled to stand, Jesus reached for his arm to steady and help him. With outstretched arms, they embraced, and in that embrace, hurt and sorrow left.

Jesus turned and knelt beside the pool, splashing cool water across his face. Refreshed, he walked slowly to the shade of the fruit tree, found a nectarine, and sat down. Moses followed suit, and soon, the two of them were engaged in lighthearted conversation as the jackal and cub parried in play on the far side of the pool. The light midmorning breeze brought a soft rustle in the overhead leaves.

"What's Michael doing today?" Moses asked. "I haven't seen him about. Are there more surprises ahead?"

"I'm sure he has his hands full at the moment," Jesus chuckled, his eyes fixed on the tumbling pair. "But that's for another day. Today, I'm hoping to gain more insight from you about a couple of things. As my time in this wilderness comes to a close, and I don't yet know how long that will be, I want to be ready for what lies ahead in my time as a man.

"A few days ago, I asked how you remained faithful to your purpose. You said it hinged on an absolute certainty it was I Am's purpose working through you, not yours, and that certainty was underscored as supernatural powers were entrusted to you. Do you remember?"

"Yes, Jesus, that is what I said," replied Moses, "and that is true."

"Okay," Jesus continued, "so that leads me to the other thing I am trying to understand—and I'm only asking so I'm ready when confronted with it. So I want to come back to that earlier question about doubt…"

Moses bristled.

"But please hear me out. I'm not asking for the sake of opening old wounds. I'm just trying to understand what causes a man to doubt his innermost convictions. At Meribah, for one brief moment, you doubted whether the power I Am had promised had failed. And so I ask—not in judgment but to understand—why did you doubt?"

Moses was focused on Jesus's demeanor. Clearly, Jesus was earnest in his query. It was as though he was anticipating some future test and trying to understand whether he could pass it. What was the answer to that question? For forty more years of wandering, he had wrestled with that very question himself. Why had he doubted I Am in that moment when I Am had always been reliably steadfast?

"Oh, how I wish I knew the answer, Jesus," Moses began. "It is a question that haunted me all my life. If only I had not doubted. If only I could back up in time and have one more chance at that moment. If only. Life is filled with 'if onlys.' Most often, they are regrets over little things. Sometimes they are life altering. That 'if only' was one of those, and it came from a moment of doubt. Why, in that moment, did I doubt I Am? In looking back on it, none of it makes sense. None of it.

"Yet you ask *why?* Maybe my resolve was weakened by exhaustion. Maybe the incessant grumbling of a million stiff-necked people had gotten to me. Maybe Aaron had doubted whether we could find water to satisfy everyone because everything seemed so hopeless. And when those closest to you begin to doubt, maybe it becomes harder to keep doubt at bay. Maybe for one brief moment I had questioned whether, in spite of all the powers I Am had demonstrated through me, well, maybe I felt somehow I Am had forsaken me. Should I have known better? Yes, of course. In that brief moment, maybe I was overwhelmed by everything around me, and my certainty was shaken."

Moses sighed. "I don't know, Jesus. I don't know. What I do know is that doubt brought deep regret afterward. Deep regret. When water gushed out of that rock after the second strike, I was overcome by regret, but I couldn't back up in time. So I lived the rest of my life wallowing in a private deep regret because for one moment, I had lost sight of the goodness of I Am." Another sigh followed, and Moses fell silent, head bowed and eyes closed. He was exhausted and emotionally spent, his bald crown glistening with tiny beads of sweat.

They sat in silence, the gentle rustle of the overhead leaves surrounding them. The jackal and cub were at rest. Jesus stared pensively at the bed of leaves beneath him, yet mindless of them. Moses's confession had moved him. He was still, pondering.

After a while, he continued softly. "I want to be ready, Moses. I want to be ready when all seems lost. I want to be ready when doubt comes."

DAY 14

Rest

On the seventh day, he rested.

DAY 15

Michael
Free Will

"How was he, when you parted?"

"Relieved, I think," Michael said, "and at peace. Moses didn't tell me what you talked about, but he seemed to be at peace with himself—and relieved to be shedding the shackles of time. I think he was grateful for the conversation, and he was pleased to learn you will probably want to see him again as a human. Of course, he continues to be curious about all this, of what is unfolding."

"As are you." Jesus chuckled.

It was early morn, sunrise just minutes away. He had found Jesus leaning against a rock at the top of the far ridge, the jackal curled at his feet. As he approached, Jesus's eyes had remained fixed on the outline of the gnarled ancient oak far in the distance. "You've been silent about your time with Storm out there," Michael noted. "Something bothering you?"

"No, nothing about the time with Storm," Jesus replied, turning toward Michael with a hint of a smile. He pondered silently for a few moments as his countenance slowly turned somber in reflection. He seemed to be struggling with how to express the divine thoughts that had him transfixed in this human-yet-divine being, this Jesus/ I Am.

"When I Am breathed and all came into being, it was purest joy to imbue the heavenly and earthly beings with the gift of free will[16]—the gift to make their own choices. That gift has brought my greatest joy and my deepest pain. I grieve when an earthly being chooses a path which will bring harm. It is difficult to let them go on that path. Indeed, you and all the heavenly hosts grieve with the I Am of me as well—and I can see the pain in you.

"The other day with the satan, I experienced the *thrill* of pondering something new to me as a man, and within that, the freedom a man feels having the power to choose. It was enlightening to learn how the satan sways the thoughts of man, how innocent it can begin, and in free will, how decisions that lead to harm can begin in such small and innocent increments.

"In my encounter with the satan—who, by the way, insisted on being called *Delilah*—it was clear the satan also exercises that free will, sometimes in ways that seem harmless, sometimes in ways to deceive. I'm not sure a human is capable of withstanding the free will which the satan exercises. And when falling into the trap of the satan's free will, even surrendering to it, the pain which humanity suffers grieves me deeply.

"It was never my intent through the gift of free will that pain and suffering would be the result, but much of human suffering begins with the oh-so-subtle yielding of one's own free will to the will of the satan. It is my deepest yearning, Michael, to reshape creation—to reshape how free will can be the joy and blessing I had intended for all."

Michael was moved by the emotion of Jesus's words and the longing in his eyes.

"That is what lies ahead, Michael," Jesus sighed, "a path to restore humanity to the joy I intended."

---

[16] Sirach 15:14

DAY 16

Michael and Gabriel
Preparing for King David

"I'm going to rest a day," Jesus had said. "The encounter with the satan has opened my eyes to his power over man—even over those with the strongest of character. I will see David tomorrow. Prepare a suitable place." Slowly he had meandered off just before dawn, surrounded by a loose array of wild creatures. He had looked tired. So after Jesus's departure Michael had assembled an army of heavenly helpers to *prepare a suitable place.*

The oasis had been transformed. The spring-fed pool was now at the hub of a bustling community. Dusty streets extended outward like spokes of a wheel, the desert emptiness no more. Clusters of Bedouin goat-hair tents of every size and shape surrounded open-air bazaars. The subtle aroma of roast lamb hung tauntingly in the air. Children at play spilled into the streets. Mothers clutching young ones clucked protectively. Old men swapped tales under the sprawl of the tamarisk trees which dotted the village. The main cobblestone avenue, lined on either side by stately date palms, stretched nearly to the horizon. Sprawling camel-hair tent palaces of clan chieftains colorfully adorned with tribe markings faced the grand avenue. It too bustled with activity. Bleating goats butted barking dogs, speckled guineas cackled at skittish cats, while children tussled over hide-covered balls, oblivious to the din around them.

As dusk neared, Jesus approached the transformed community in awe and delight. With rest had come the return of laughter and lightheartedness. As the settlement neared, the entourage of wild creatures that had entertained and comforted him during the day gradually drifted away. Only the pup and its falcon nemesis remained.

The stroll from the village edge along the grand avenue to the village hub was uneventful. The jackal pup nipped playfully at guinea and goat along the way, while the falcon claimed Jesus's shoulder, its head swiveling now and then, which underscored a regal bearing. Occasionally a chieftain in colorful robe and headdress would cast a glance in their direction, stretch an arm, and point. His eyes and those around him were fixed on the kingly falcon, all the while ignoring the unassuming stranger in the simple tunic.

Jesus recognized Michael's dark cloak from a distance. He was sitting on a stone bench at the pool in deep conversation with a man of similar build also in dark cloak. Jesus paused. Even from afar, something about the second man was familiar.

Sensing a change, the young jackal's eyes turned toward the cloaked ones, and at the same moment, the falcon leapt downward. The game was on to the surprise of the nearby children who squealed in delight at each swooping tease. Excitement and laughter filled the air. A crowd soon gathered along the avenue, enthralled by the springing pup and the agile falcon at the center of its attention. Waves of laughter followed each near miss of the jackal's frenzied leaps.

Curiosity aroused, Michael and his friend stood and turned toward the laughter. With wide grins, both men waved in welcome. Jesus smiled and returned the wave and continued walking toward the pool. With the game over, the falcon lazily looped higher and higher toward the pool and the shade of its familiar fruit tree. The pup too set off toward the pool at an easy trot. Jesus followed casually, enjoying the bustle as children and animals returned to their play.

"Ah, Gabriel." Jesus smiled as he approached. The two men embraced warmly. "It is good to see you." There were similarities to Michael. Both were of average height and muscular build, with strong chins and dark confident eyes, but Gabriel's hair was longer, dark and wavy, speckled with gray. And unlike Michael's bronze skin,

Gabriel was more ebony than bronze. "Michael said he was going to get some help, but I wasn't expecting this. Have you enjoyed the day?"

Gabriel stepped back, looked Jesus up and down, and reached for the water cup on the nearby stone. "Yes, today has been fun. First, you could use a drink." He handed Jesus the cup. "From the looks of it, you've been in the desert all day. And you're back just in time for supper. One of the families has invited us for lamb stew and bread. We were just setting out."

Jesus drank slowly from the cup and then turned toward Michael. "I delight in your surprises, Michael." He smiled. "When I said *prepare a suitable place*, I wasn't expecting anything like this." His expression was a mixture of curiosity and satisfaction as he slowly pivoted to survey Michael's handiwork. "A whole village? It is spectacular, and it pleases me. Yet I don't understand. Why a village?"

Michael grinned. "All right, a quick explanation, then you've got to get cleaned up for supper. You can't go like that. You look like a walking dust devil! You'll scare the kids and the dogs to death!" Michael swatted his tunic, and the three roared with laughter at Jesus as the cloud of dust rose around him.

"Fair enough," Jesus laughed. "I'll clean up, but tell me about this village."

"It was Gabriel's idea. I asked Gabriel to find David and bring him here, but it seems David wasn't too excited about stepping back into time, even though he is intrigued about you as a man. So he put conditions on his coming."

"Conditions!" Jesus exclaimed. "What does that mean? Who is he to set conditions on coming at my direction?" He turned to Gabriel. "Did you tell him who was calling him?" Jesus was not amused at the grin on Gabriel's face. "What's so funny? Did you tell him? Did you make it clear?"

Gabriel caught himself, forcing a serious tone. "Sure, I told him," he said. "He wasn't disrespectful. He just said that if he was going to step back into time again as a man, he'd like some adulation as part of it. So when I told Michael, we cooked up the idea of a village to welcome him when he arrives."

Jesus turned to Michael who could not conceal his delight at Jesus's consternation. "This is for David's benefit, this village?" he exclaimed, gesturing over his shoulder to the village around them. "You put this together so there'd be *adulation*?" Jesus was caught short!

"Well, you said *prepare a suitable place,*" Michael smirked. "David wants adulation—we'll give him adulation."

"And all the people?" Jesus asked. "What's with all the people? What have they been told?"

"Ah, that's the best part. Michael thinks of everything. They are all heavenly hosts who have been watching you since your birth in Bethlehem. They were excited about the chance to experience time. So they're here as humans as long as David is with us, but in this human state, they don't know anything about you. They only know that King David is coming tomorrow, and they're very excited they will get to see the king. David wants adulation? He's going to get adulation," Gabriel exclaimed.

Jesus stared at them, incredulous, first Michael, then Gabriel, then back to Michael. Their faces feigned sobriety, but their eyes betrayed their glee. "You two! You are enjoying this far too much. We'll talk more after supper. Much more." With that, Jesus spun around and strode to the wash bowl nearby.

Gabriel nudged Michael, and they both grinned. Jesus's reaction was better than they had imagined.

DAY 17

Morning
David—Royal Arrival

His tent was nearest the pool on the dusty street two spokes away from the grand avenue. It was simple, befitting the unassuming stranger. Last night's host had stopped by earlier and given Michael some fresh cakes and baked lamb for breakfast, while Gabriel had picked some figs and nectarines. Breakfast around the low table had been satisfying and delicious. Now Jesus was alone, reclining just inside the tent and absently watching the activity around the pool. The village was slowly coming to life as predawn light signaled the coming day. He could see Michael seated on the far side of the pool, fully attentive to a couple of silk-robed chieftains engaged in spirited conversation. Though the trio was too distant for Jesus to understand words, flourishing arms and hands conveyed their excitement.

The sound of rapidly approaching footsteps grew, until suddenly, Gabriel burst into the tent. "Where's Michael?" he gasped, looking past Jesus and around the tent. Jesus smiled and nodded. "Well, where is he?" Gabriel panted. Jesus nodded to the pool, pointing toward Michael.

Gabriel turned, spied Michael, and ran to him and the two chieftains. Flourishing arms dropped to their sides as they listened to what the second cloaked one had to say. Michael rose, turned briefly to look at Jesus, and then back to the leaders. After a few words, their gaze fixed on Jesus for a few moments. Bowing respectfully to

Michael and Gabriel, the two men left quickly along the grand avenue toward their tribal tents. Excitement hinged on the news from the two cloaked strangers: King David was near!

*****

"Well, he had to tell them *something*," Gabriel exclaimed. "They are of course excited that King David is coming to their village, but they wanted to know why. So Michael told them he would be here to see a distant relative about a family matter. They want to host a feast and celebration in his honor, but we explained he wouldn't have time—that he's come only for a brief private visit with you."

"And they accepted that?" Jesus frowned.

"Grudgingly, yes." Michael smiled. "Though they found it peculiar that you don't appear to come from a royal line. Even so, they have promised to respect the privacy you seek. The word has already gone out that the king is near. In fact," he said, turning his gaze toward the horizon beyond the cobblestone avenue, "judging from the cloud of dust, it looks like his army is approaching." He turned. "Go Gabriel, and meet him at the village edge as agreed. We will wait for you here."

"Army?" Jesus exclaimed. "His army? Why an army?"

"Gabriel told him he could bring some friends," Michael smirked. "Just for the day. It's all part of the adulation. Don't worry. They'll be encamped beyond the village."

Jesus sighed. "You're enjoying this, aren't you, Michael," he said, rolling his eyes.

"Maybe a little," Michael chuckled, "and Gabriel liked it. He's looking forward to being King David's personal escort."

"Well, have your fun. I'll be waiting," Jesus replied as he stepped inside the tent. "This could take a while, so I think I'll take a nap. Rouse me when he's here." He closed the tent flap behind him. Michael grinned.

*****

Weaving through the noisy throng, it took Gabriel longer than he anticipated to reach the end of the avenue. With chieftains barking instructions, the excited crowd gathered palm fronds and spread brightly colored cloaks to carpet the center of the avenue. Soon the colorful carpet and waving fronds stretched its entire length to greet the approaching royalty.

King David rode erect atop the ebony stallion, entranced by the growing din of jubilant villagers with the steady cadence of the advancing army behind him. The steed was magnificent. Black eyes danced and nostrils flared as its muscular frame glistened under the desert sun. Silver medallions accented the black leather bridle and royal-blue riding blanket. Weaving back and forth in spirited canter along the line of the advancing troops, it slowed to a crisp, high-stepping walk at the master's command. Turning toward the village, he and the master moved as one.

David bore the confidence of a returning warrior fresh after victory, muscular and bronzed by the Mediterranean sun. Dark gray eyes missed nothing. Courage lined his brow, accented by a strong clean-shaven jaw. With every turn of the horse, dark wavy hair brushed the nape of his neck. A black leather vest open to the waist complemented the pleated warrior skirt and sandals, all tastefully adorned in silver. Hanging loosely from his neck, the silver chain with its six-point medallion adorned the broad bare chest. He sat easily astride the stallion, his muscular legs firmly gripping its barrel.

Leaving the village behind, Gabriel strode briskly to the entourage and bowed deeply as the king approached. Raising one hand and reining the horse with the other, both crowd and cadence fell silent. Rising to his full height, Gabriel proclaimed, "Welcome, mighty king! We bow humbly before you." As one, the crowd bowed and then erupted in jubilation. King David beamed and nodded to receive their cries.

Turning, the king motioned the army to remain in place. He dismounted and turned back to Gabriel. "Take me to him," he commanded above the cries of the crowd. "Where is he?"

Gabriel leaned close. "Your Majesty," he cried, "please proceed before me to the village center along the avenue which has been prepared. You will find him there. For now, the people await you." Gabriel swept his arm to the cloak-strewn avenue and the palm-waving crowd and bowed deeply. The king strode to the village entrance, paused, and stepped onto the cloak-laden cobblestone. All along the way, the crowd strewed palm fronds in his path while bowing and proclaiming, "Hail, O mighty king." Ever so slowly he progressed, joyfully reveling in their adulation. As he passed by, the crowd followed in jubilant celebration.

*****

"This is a bit much," Jesus groaned. The din of the crowd grew as David progressed closer to the village center. Soon it was overpowering. Jesus pulled the flap aside and peered out. Michael was standing just beyond the flap in front of the tent. The excitement of the crowd—the cheering, the jubilation—was at fever pitch. As the crowd slowly parted to make way for the king, Jesus first glimpsed Gabriel. And then David. They paused at the foot of the avenue beside the pool. David turned to face the crowd and raised his arms to acknowledge their cheers. The crowd erupted. Adulation had reached its peak.

Michael slowly strode toward Gabriel and leaned close to speak in his ear. Their dark cloaks stood in deep contrast to the bright silken robes of the chieftains and the sand-colored tunics of their tribes. "Enough, Gabriel," he cried over the din. "It's time."

Gabriel's dark features glistened as he approached David from the rear and spoke into his ear. He turned, and with a wave of his cloak, Gabriel stepped onto the stone bench at the pool's edge. Raising both arms, the crowd slowly quieted as King David turned away from the crowd to face him.

"Welcome home, mighty king!" Gabriel proclaimed. The crowd erupted anew in a sustained frenzy. After a time, Gabriel again raised his arms, and the crowd fell silent. "The king is grateful for your warm welcome," he declared. "Now he must tend to the royal matter before him. So return to your home with his blessing. Long live King David!" Once again, the crowd erupted. David turned toward them and waved to acknowledge the adulation. Then he turned and approached Michael.

"Where is he?" he asked. "Is he near?" He was surveying the splendor of the nearby chieftain's elaborate dwelling.

"Closer than you know," Michael demurred, "closer than you know." He turned and started toward the simple shepherd's tent at the foot of the gravel path nearby. David followed while Gabriel remained behind dispersing the crowd. When the crowd had diminished, Gabriel turned and found Michael sitting at the pool alone. The flap of the nearby tent was closed. All was quiet.

*****

It was a shepherd's tent after all, David reminisced, the cloth breaking the wind but little else. Even with the flap closed, filtered daylight pleasantly filled the space. At the center lay a flat stone on which rested a couple of goblets, a wine flask, and a loaf of bread. On either side lay two plain pillows; a man was half reclined on one. He rose and stretched his arms in greeting as David entered. In two strides, David returned the greeting as they embraced.

"Quite a welcome Michael and Gabriel came up with." Jesus smiled. "Was it what you had hoped for?"

"A little over the top, huh?" David grinned. "When Michael came to tell me you would see me here, I thought I'd take advantage of it. *If I'm going to step back into time,* I said, *it would be nice to be adored by my people again.* I guess he took it as a challenge. And I must say, he and Gabriel surprised even me! The army, and the village, and the stallion? Even my old medallion," he exclaimed, lifting the star for Jesus to admire. "Very impressive, indeed!"

"Come," Jesus invited and, sitting, gestured to the other pillow. "Rest with me and let your memories flow while I explain why you are here." Taking the flask, Jesus poured the wine. "You must be hungry too," he said, breaking the bread and offering it and the wine to David.

Removing his sandals and vest, David moved to the pillow. Slowly sipping the wine, he reflected, "Ah, that is better than I remember. Much better." He paused to let the wine blossom, then nibbled on the offered morsel. "Fine wine and freshly-baked bread." He sighed as he returned the goblet to the stone, closed his eyes, and fully reclined. Silence filled the air. Jesus smiled as David's breathing slowed. The return to time always had that effect, so a brief nap was normal.

DAY 17

Afternoon
David—Adulation, Pride, Power

The door flap hung loosely, an occasional wisp of the early-afternoon breeze cooling the tent. The village was quiet. David stirred.

"Feeling better?" Jesus asked. "After thirty years, I'm used to the effect of time, but Michael and Gabriel have reminded me that it can be a difficult adjustment. We're in no hurry, so rest easy."

David sat up, rubbed his eyes, tossed his fingers through his hair, and stretched, a long head-to-toe stretch. "Ahhh, the memory of a sound sleep. That is a gift!" The chalice soon found his lips, the sip of wine bringing a smile. "Excellent," he sighed softly. His gaze turned to Jesus, who was reclined on his side, watching him.

"So why am I here? What's this all about? Michael is confused and wasn't any help. So why am I here?"

"At the right time, Michael will know—and so will you," Jesus said softly. "At the right time. But these days in the wilderness are a time for me to explore the nature of humans and the nature of the satan. When I Am created humanity in the divine image, humanity received the gift of free will—just as the heavenly beings did. The gift of free will has been a delight, but at times, it has been a cause of divine sorrow. When choices bring harm, I Am grieves. And though grief can be very deep, I Am remains steadfast to the gift of free will. It is free will which distinguishes humanity from all other earthly creatures—by reflecting the divine image. And divine steadfastness means poor human choices never diminish the depth of I Am's love—no matter what."

David sat very still, intent on Jesus's every word.

"Surely Michael has told you that I have been speaking with a number of persons, yes?"

"Yes, he has," David replied. "He also told me you have met with the satan—or *Storm*, I think he called him—but he doesn't know why."

Jesus chuckled. "Yes, poor Michael. He is very curious. He has figured this much out: that as a man, as Jesus, the time ahead will bring me face-to-face with choices—with free will—and in those choices, face-to-face with the nature of the satan and the ways of the satan in and through humanity. During these next days, I want to learn from others who have fought with the urges of the satan so I can be ready for those urges. So I will prevail when they come."

Now David was intrigued. "So you have met with the satan— with Storm. What have you learned?"

"Ah, a timely question indeed," Jesus reflected. "I learned that for a human, it is very difficult to resist the allure of lust. That what begins in innocence—the attraction of one to another—can turn quickly when the satan subverts the purity of the natural urges for his ends. When the thirst for physical satisfaction trumps the best interests of the other, those urges can prompt behaviors which are contrary to I Am's designed beauty of intimacy. Even the most resolute cannot stand against the will of the satan."

"So, Jesus, my past comes back to haunt me, does it?" David asked, one eyebrow raised. "Why single me out? The physical desire for another runs throughout the history of man—that thirst for sexual satisfaction. Surely you have seen its effect on a man—surely you have felt that dull throb in your loins, that gnawing hunger for natural pleasure. Every man has or will at some point." David's eyes didn't betray his curiosity. His questions were more accusatory than inquisitive. "It seems your observation comes from the voice of experience. Have you ever satisfied that hunger? Have you known a woman?"

Jesus studied David's face, letting his words hang in the air. David's stare didn't waver. "Have you?" David repeated. Only the sound of their shallow breathing disturbed the stillness.

Slowly, Jesus rose and turned toward the flap. "Let's take a walk," he said as he tossed the flap open and stepped outside. David followed.

The village was gone. Only desert wilderness stretched away on one side with the pool and the tree on the other. No villagers, no chieftains. No Michael, no Gabriel. They were alone. No distractions. Jesus smiled. *Michael knows me too well*, he thought. He turned toward the distant horizon in a casual stroll with the midday sun behind, beckoning David to come alongside for lighthearted conversation. David regaled Jesus with stories from his shepherd youth, how as the youngest in a band of bantering brothers he often had to endure the brunt of sibling rivalry.

"What about the day Samuel came and sized up your brothers and then picked you last for anointing as the future king?"[17] Jesus asked with delight. "How did that go over?"

"With my brothers, not very well." David grinned. "If anything, the teasing got worse. That's the way it is being the kid brother. The ribbing was relentless after Samuel left. Yeah, Dad was proud. My brothers? Oh boy…relentless!

"Of course, that all changed with the Philistines and the Goliath thing.[18] That celebration was unreal, how everyone was slapping me on the back, hoisting me up and tossing me in the air, shouting my name, cheering—sheer jubilation. Of course, I loved it. I think that was the first time my brothers felt slighted, even slighted by Dad. All the attention was on me. They never said anything, but things were different after that. Even King Saul was jubilant that day. I must confess, I loved being at the center of it all, everybody yelling my name. All of a sudden, I was important—and people would part to make way for me when I went into the village. It sure beat herding sheep!" he exclaimed.

---

[17] 1 Samuel 16:1–13
[18] 1 Samuel 17:4–51

They meandered aimlessly for several hours, leading to a gentle rise as David delighted in sharing stories of conquest, tempered by the memories of King Saul fearing his loss of power, the king's pursuit of David as his reputation grew and, tenderly, of the special relationship with Jonathan, the king's son.[19]

"He was my deepest friend," his voice trembled, tear-filled eyes absently fixed beyond the horizon. "In truth, after his death, the pain was unbearable. My heart never recovered. From then on, I didn't allow myself to become as intimate of soul with another person—man or woman. I could not endure the deep pain again." He fell silent.

They had approached an outcropping, a tuft of greenery at its base. Nodding toward it, Jesus said softly, "Let's rest in the shade for a while." From a small crack halfway up its face, a rivulet trickled to the foot and disappeared underground. They took turns cupping hands into the slow trickle, finding refreshment from the sun and dust. The shadow from the outcropping brought just enough shelter from the searing heat for the patch of desert grass to survive. Jesus sat to one side of the trickle, bare feet enjoying the soft grass, with his back propped against the rock. David lay on his back, staring into the cloudless sky. High above, an eagle looped lazily in the desert updrafts. Rest brought serenity, the soft steady trickle of the spring-fed rivulet the only sound.

*****

"You enjoyed it, didn't you?" Jesus asked quietly, eyes fixed on the distant eagle. He hadn't moved, still reclined against the rock. The leisurely flow of conversation had been pleasant. Jesus seemed to hang on every word, which pleased David. He could recall others feigning interest during his reign as king, but eventually, their interest proved to be self-serving. Jesus's was different—his interest was genuine. In the quiet, David had lowered his guard. Where would this question lead?

---

[19] 2 Samuel 1:25–26

"Enjoyed what?" he asked, turning his gaze toward Jesus.

"The adulation," Jesus continued. "You enjoyed the adulation this morning, and the adulation which came with being king. Am I right?"

He could feel the warmth at the back of his neck. "So what if I did?" David responded testily. "Is there anything wrong with that? After all, I *earned* it, and some would say I *deserved* it." He was caught by surprise at the question, and his defenses kicked in. His eyes narrowed as small beads of sweat dampened his brow. He stood and turned his back to Jesus to gather his composure. "So what if I did?" he repeated, staring into the distance, an iciness in his tone.

Jesus calmly turned his head, eyeing the tension in David's stance. He was bemused by the strong reaction to such an innocent question. It seemed out of character. Slowly, the tension subsided, and David's earlier demeanor returned. From a slow pivot, he studied Jesus for a moment and then casually sat on the grass. The silence was awkward.

Jesus broke the silence. "Were you good at shepherding?" David looked at him quizzically. "Of all Jesse's boys, who was the best at shepherding?" Jesus rephrased. "Why did your father pick you, his youngest son, to care for and protect his flock?" he asked reflectively. Then slowly he continued, "Why do you think he picked you?"

Now David was confused. "I never gave it much thought, to be honest," he replied. "I mean, I never wondered why Dad picked me to tend the flock on any given day. We all took our turns, or at least that's what I remember."

"Were you good at it?" Jesus repeated thoughtfully, his eyes once again on the eagle in its lazy loops. "Were you good at shepherding?"

David's eyes turned to the eagle as well. "Yeah, I guess I was good at it. Or at least my dad must have thought so. Otherwise, he wouldn't have sent me out there. The flock was very important to us."

"Were you better than any of your brothers?" Jesus probed.

David smiled. "Well, I like to think I was—and I think Dad thought so too. In the village when the men gathered, he enjoyed their sense that the flock seemed to fare better under my watch. He was proud of his flock. And you could tell by the way his eyes danced, he was proud of me too."

"How did that make you feel?" Jesus was listening intently, though his attention seemed riveted overhead. "And why do you think the villagers thought you were the better shepherd?"

"How did it make me feel?" David reflected, recalling those days of youth. "Every boy wants to do well in his father's eyes and make him proud. I guess in making my dad proud, it made me proud. I was proud that the village men knew me, that they admired my skill. Why did they think I was the better shepherd? Because I was!"

With arms folded across his chest, he continued, "Everybody knew that. And those skills came in pretty handy when Goliath came along. Then they *knew* just how skilled I was! Even King Saul knew how good I was. From then on, I never gave another thought to how I compared to my brothers. The cheers of the soldiers and villagers—of everyone now free of living in fear of the Philistine giant—well, there was no question about who was the better shepherd. It was as though the villagers had become my flock, and I had slain the wild beast. Now the whole village knew of my skills! And it wasn't long after that, my shepherding days were over. I was very good at what I did. As my warrior reputation grew, so did my pride. And many would tell you that it was well deserved." Chest and arm muscles flexed and glistened as he spoke, a hint of boastfulness in his tone. David's eyes were firmly set on Jesus.

Jesus sat silently, absently focused on the distant eagle but attentive to David's every word. With an air of impatience, David relaxed his arms and sat. The silence continued. After a few moments, he broke the silence. "Were you listening to me?" he asked impatiently.

Still Jesus's gaze remained on the soaring eagle as it slowly rose higher and higher in ever-widening loops. David followed his gaze, exasperated by the silence. One loop. Two loops.

Halfway through its third loop, Jesus mused softly, "Which comes first, adulation or pride?" It was as though he was thinking out loud. "Does one follow the other? If so, which comes first?" Now his gaze slowly turned to David. "Do you remember?"

"What difference does it make which comes first?" David replied testily.

*****

The sound of distant footsteps interrupted them. Both turned to see the lone figure approaching in a rapid gait. "I wasn't sure I would be able to find you," Michael panted anxiously. "I didn't see you leave, but the footprints in the sand helped." He was out of breath, clad only in a loincloth, the desert dust caked in head-to-toe perspiration.

"Sit, my friend." Jesus waved his arm in invitation. "Enjoy some cool water and tell us what brings you in such haste." Michael knelt beside the cool trickle and gathered handful after handful, splashing his brow and satisfying his thirst.

"It's Storm," he said at last, alarmed. "He insists on meeting you by evening at the old oak. Something about *unfinished business*." The breathing was coming easier. "He wouldn't tell me what it was about. He just said you would know." His breathing slowed further. "When I asked if it could wait, he erupted." He turned to Jesus, ignoring David. "What's going on?" he asked, confused and clearly worried.

David was intrigued, focused on Jesus's expression. "The satan wants to see Jesus *now*?" he repeated, incredulity in his voice. "*Unfinished business*? That's strange." He paused. "I'm with Michael on this one. What's going on?"

Jesus chuckled as his eyes danced. "Storm's in a hurry, huh, and has something to say?" He laughed. "I'll bet he does." He was clearly enjoying this moment and the reactions of Michael and David. He stood slowly and stretched, a slow arching stretch, breathing deeply. He jangled his arms, flexed his knees, twisted his head from side to side, and sat. Michael was perplexed; David, curious.

Jesus lay back on the ground, eyes returning to the distant eagle. "Go back, Michael—and tell Storm I'm busy. And tell him when I'm ready to see him again, you will make the arrangements as before."

"You're toying with me, right?" Michael responded. "You want me to go back and tell Storm that you'll see him when you get around to it?" He was on edge. "If that's what you want me to do, I'm not going to be in any hurry returning. I can only imagine Storm's reaction. For whatever reason, he seems to be in a hurry. He's not going to like being put off." He glanced at David. "Hey, I know. How about you send David, instead?"

Jesus laughed and rolled on his side, eyes on Michael. "Oh, all right, Michael. Tell Storm I'll meet him under the old oak in three days. It will be interesting to see what he wants and why he is in such a hurry." He smiled. "But take as long as you want going back." He paused in thought. "One more thing. I want to spend some time with Bathsheba tomorrow. Would you invite her to the pool under the fruit tree, please?" He turned toward David. "And no special effects this time," he smirked.

David's eyes widened in discomfort. Jesus's instruction had unsettled him. "Bathsheba? Why her? What do you want with her?"

"Rest as long as you like, Michael," Jesus said. "You have things to do." He turned to David. "We have more to talk about."

*****

Michael had left at a slow walk; now silence surrounded them. The instruction about Bathsheba had David on edge. Jesus's gaze had returned to follow the eagle.

"Where were we?" Jesus began. "Ah, yes. I was intrigued by your story and was wondering which came first in your experience: adulation or pride? Whether one follows the other, and if so, which comes first." He turned to David. "Your reply was short, as I recall. Something like, 'What difference does it make, which comes first?' Something about that bothers you."

"What do you want with Bathsheba?" David blurted, ignoring Jesus's attempt to return to the earlier conversation. "There is nothing you can learn from her that I can't tell you. Ask me anything you want," he pressed. "Why waste your time with her?"

"You, my friend, have nothing to fear," Jesus replied. "Your past is in the past and long ago forgotten. I didn't bring you back to dig up old wounds."

A wave of relief swept over David. He sat silently for a few moments, then turned to Jesus's question. "I'm not sure it matters," he began, "whether adulation or pride comes first." He stopped, reflecting, and then continued, "Maybe pride. In my shepherd days, especially in the early years when dad and my brothers taught me some of the tricks to protect the flock and keep it together, like using the rod to defend against the wolf or lion and the sling to keep them at a distance or how to gather the lambs with the staff when they strayed, I guess as time went by, I felt pride in learning those skills, at being better than anybody else. Just pride in knowing I was good at it.

"There was no adulation then. If there was, maybe it was self-adulation, but I don't think so. I was just proud I had learned well. And when I saw the pride in my dad's eyes as he watched me, I felt proud. He never said anything, but I could see the pride in his eyes—the pride a father feels for his son." He paused. "Surely you have felt that pride at learning the skills taught by your earthly father, Joseph, haven't you? And when he smiled with pride as he watched your handiwork at the lathe, didn't you feel pride too?"

Jesus smiled as his thoughts turned to those days. "Yes, those feelings, when you see the pride in your father's eyes, those feelings shape a boy as he passes through youth to manhood. It's good for me to remember those days. Thank you," he reflected. "Yet the quiet pride—the unspoken adulation in a father's eyes—is different from the kind of adulation that can change the nature of a man, the kind of adulation you craved when Michael approached you for our time together. The obedient army, the cheering throngs, how does that kind of adulation affect a man? What becomes of pride then?"

David was silent, staring across the desert wasteland, as though studying himself in a mirror. Jesus lay still on his side, watching David. "That is most interesting," David began slowly, mulling his thoughts over in his mind. "The pride and adulation we've been talking about seems to me is born of the innocence of childhood. So when does that innocence begin to give way to other influences? And where do those influences come from?" His vacant stare continued.

"I mentioned the exhilaration in slaying Goliath. Maybe it was then that childhood innocence wavered. The celebration of the people—and their adulation—caused a different kind of pride now that I think about it. Maybe it was then the shift began. It is difficult to describe. Maybe a boastful pride, not overtly boastful but an underlying feeling of exceptional accomplishment, of stepping forward in innocence to do something that everyone else had cowered from. And then once the task was complete, a different kind of pride ensued as the roars, the ovations, grew. All the attention shifted to *me*, a kind of attention that was new to me. And for the first time, I actually liked the attention—the adulation. Something had changed—the way the people now saw me, the way I saw myself. All of a sudden, I was no longer the shepherd boy. In their eyes, I became a warrior, a mighty warrior, for having slayed *their* mighty threat.

"From that moment, the story spread throughout the land, and my reputation went before me. The more the stories were repeated, the greater the warrior I became. And I liked it. I liked it when runners ran ahead to alert people I was coming—-and the crowds gathered shouting their praise and admiration as I entered their village. The innocence of boyhood pride was no more. It had become a puffed-up pride, a boastful pride. As stories were told and retold, I became greater than life. The more I heard those stories, the more *I* believed them." David paused, taking a long, slow deep breath, his vacant eyes still fixed on the desert wasteland. "I'm beginning to see myself in a different way, and I'm not proud of what I am seeing," he said softly as though to himself. He turned to Jesus. "So what kind of pride is *that*—of not being proud of what I'm seeing? Maybe a belated return to innocence?"

Jesus hadn't stirred, his eyes and attention riveted on David. While David seemed to be seeking a response, Jesus remained silent. "It was the little things," David continued. "As I think back, it was the little things at the beginning that caused the change. After Goliath, it was as though everything I did—even the little things—were deemed large by the people. They were hungry for a warrior to lead them, to conquer the enemies all around, to bring peace to their anxious lives.

"After the death of King Saul, and I became king of all the people, the adulation was all around. As our armies conquered in battle after battle, the fervor in the crowd in every village fueled my pride. Everyone—friend or foe—knew who King David was. The adulation of my people and the respect of every foe signaled the stature of my position and the power of my word. At my word, people would act. I no longer had to raise a sword with a mighty arm. My power was in my presence and my word.

"So," David reflected, "it seems pride led to adulation and respect, and adulation and respect led to power. Of the three—pride, adulation, power—power was the most satisfying. With power, nothing stands in your way. Power exhilarates like nothing else. It satisfies beyond the finest wine."

Jesus had been still, focused on David and his every word. In this time of wilderness separation, Jesus had hoped to explore the nature of power and its influence on the behavior of man. Unknowingly, David had brought them there, and now David had turned silent, still staring across the desert emptiness. Silence surrounded them, both reflecting on David's words.

"I never gave this any thought, Jesus, until now," David continued. "But as I reflect on the experience of entering the village yesterday, I wonder. Those villagers Michael and Gabriel assembled were very typical. The praise, the adulation—they gave it freely. When people are downtrodden, when despair or want consumes them, they are willing to submit to any power they think will bring them a future that is better than their past or better than their present. Even people who have much but are not satisfied with their abundance will submit to power if they believe that in doing so, they will receive even more. So it seems power can be the result of a craving—a craving of the people wanting more or of a leader craving personal satisfaction or the adulation of the multitudes." He paused. "Of the three, power can be the most dangerous because the one wielding it can become insensitive and callous," he concluded.

Jesus rolled onto his back, his eyes searching for the distant eagle. "You enjoyed the privilege of power as king, didn't you?" he asked.

"Of course, I enjoyed it," David replied, still staring over the wasteland. "When power consumes you, you begin to believe you are bigger than you are. And that is when it becomes dangerous."

"As when you ordered Uriah the Hittite to his death so that you could have his wife, Bathsheba?"[20] Jesus queried.

David jerked to his feet, glaring at Jesus. "Is this the part of my past we were going to leave there?" he blurted, his eyes hardened. "Is that what this is all about? Has this been your game, to bring me back to my deepest regret, to my deepest grief?"

Jesus turned back to him, tenderness in his eyes. "No, David, not to revisit that part of your past. Only to seek to understand how power can consume and change the character of a man—any man— even the most honorable," he replied with sincerity. "How can a man resist that, and how will I when it comes?"

Slowly, David sank to his knees. "I wish I knew the answers to those questions, Jesus, but I don't. Maybe you should explore that in your visit with Storm. Why does a man turn from what is right to what is wrong—whether in the smallest of thoughts or the harshest of actions? That struggle is as old as creation, seems to me. I'll bet Storm has a thought or two on that."

"I'm sure he does," Jesus said softly. "I'm sure he does."

---

[20] 2 Samuel 11:14–17

DAY 18

Bathsheba
Subjugation

"Where's Michael, Gabriel?" Jesus asked. "It's not like him to sleep this late, and I haven't seen him since he found me talking with David yesterday. Do you know where he is?"

"He wasn't in a good mood when he left," Gabriel replied. "Something about a storm. He just told me to arrange for Bathsheba to be here today. 'Nothing fancy,' he said. And then he headed off over that ridge." He turned and pointed toward the earlier sunrise. "He took a couple loaves of bread, a flask, and a blanket, so I guess he's planning to be gone for a day or two. He wasn't very talkative!" He paused, turning back to Jesus. "What's going on?"

"He's on another mission, Gabriel." Jesus smiled. "Were you here before he left to find David and me?"

"No, not before he left to find you," Gabriel replied. "After you and David set out, he thanked me for my help and said my work was done, so I left. Later, I was told to meet him here and that's when he told me to arrange for Bathsheba's visit today."

"Ah, so he didn't tell you about the satan's visit." Jesus grinned. "Well, he's delivering my reply, so that's probably the reason for his sour mood. Michael is faithful and dependable—as are you, Gabriel—but he doesn't like confronting the satan. He wasn't looking forward to it, yet I haven't heard any thunder, so maybe it wasn't so bad."

"Oh, I see," Gabriel smirked. "*That* was the storm he was fearing." He smiled.

"I guess so," Jesus replied thoughtfully. After a couple of moments, he continued, "So is Bathsheba here?"

Gabriel nodded. "Maybe you haven't noticed the terebinth trees over there." He pointed in the opposite direction to a grove halfway to the horizon. "She asked for terebinths. Funny, she said the same thing Michael said, 'Nothing fancy,' just some shade and a light breeze." He turned back to Jesus. "I threw in the cushions, a basin of water, and the wine." He smiled. "A little hospitality never hurts."

Jesus turned somber. "Has she said anything about her time here?"

"Not really," Gabriel reflected. "Her beauty speaks for itself."

Jesus raised an eyebrow. "What does that mean, 'her beauty speaks for itself.' What do you mean by that?"

"You'll see," Gabriel replied.

*****

The sandals and light tunic were comfortable in the light breeze. The young jackal was enjoying the casual stroll toward the distant grove. Laughter and excited yips filled the air as Jesus danced to avoid the feigned nips at his heels. The grove was just ahead.

Bathsheba smiled in quiet delight at the distant game. As he neared, her soft giggles betrayed a serious air. A startled hare leapt from the shade of a small shrub and flitted in jagged bounds across the desert floor toward the distant horizon. The pup yelped with excitement and bolted in pursuit as both disappeared in a cloud of dust. Bathsheba's green eyes danced in merriment, accented by a smile and presence of stunning beauty.

She was sitting upright on the cushion, knees bent and legs crossed. Gently cropped, softly curled black hair with specks of gray framed a dark olive-skinned face—every feature seemingly sculpted to perfection. As he approached, Bathsheba stood and bowed deeply. She straightened, her brow just below his eyes, hands clasped at the waist, eyes downcast out of respect. Dark slender arms disappeared into the cream-colored silk blouse complemented by a loose-fitting linen wrap. The wrap hung comfortably, nearly to her ankles, revealing bejeweled, manicured nails. In the vagaries of the soft breeze, the blouse and wrap accented an exquisitely proportioned body. *Gabriel was right*, Jesus thought. *Her beauty speaks for itself.*

"Thank you for coming, Bathsheba," he said, extending his hand in greeting. "Have you been waiting long?"

"Not long, Master," she replied quietly, her head bowed slightly and eyes downcast. "It has been delightful to be within time again and to see wild creatures at play." She smiled. "It seems you have a friend in the young jackal."

"Yes, that pup is a playful one. She has a knack for making me laugh at just the right time." He chuckled.

With no acknowledgment of his outstretched hand other than an awkward silence, Jesus invited softly, "Bathsheba, will you accept my hand in welcome? And may I look into your eyes?" The meekness of her countenance moved him.

"Master," she replied tentatively, "is it not most unusual to extend such invitation to a woman? Is it not against all customs?" She was uncertain, her confusion genuine. "Yet if it is your command. it will be so." She paused. "Is that your desire?"

"It is my desire," he replied softly, "and to look into your eyes as we speak."

Slowly, she lifted her eyes and received his hand in hers. He held it tenderly and studied her face, a face of elegant beauty. Dark lashes framed the eyes, and firm cheekbones curved gracefully to the delicate yet dignified chin. Her lips were parted in a slight smile, echoing the uncertainty in her eyes. Even so, she conveyed an air of quiet confidence.

"Do you know who I am, Bathsheba, and why you are here?" he asked. "What has Gabriel told you?"

"I was told, Master, that you are the All Powerful—here as a man. That you wish to speak with me. And that you wish to be called *Jesus*." She paused, her eyes fully engaged with his. "That is all I know." Releasing his hand, she bowed gracefully. "I am at your mercy."

"Please make yourself comfortable," he said, gesturing to the cushions. She returned to her cushion, sitting upright. "Gabriel thought the wine would be refreshing. Would you like some?" He reached for a goblet.

"Ah, wine." She smiled. "Yes, that would be nice. Will you join me?" She took the chalice.

"In a moment," he said. He knelt beside the water basin, moistened the nearby cloth, removed his sandals, and began to wash the sand and dust from his feet.

"No, Master," Bathsheba quickly stood, came to his side, and knelt. "That is my duty. Please allow me."

"You are kind, Bathsheba." He smiled. "In our time together, there are some truths to guide us. So please call me Jesus. And we are here as two human beings—you as a woman, I as a man—talking with each other as equals. No master, no servant. And as equals, we honor the other by engaging openly in mutual trust—without fear. Can you accept these truths?" His eyes were fixed on hers.

"Yes, Jesus, if that is your desire," she replied. "Even so, will you accept my hospitality by allowing me to wash your feet? Yes, I am here as your guest, but will you allow me this one small privilege?"

Jesus smiled. "If it will make you happy," he relented, handing her the cloth. He leaned back on his elbows, admiring her beauty as she washed his feet. She returned to the cushion, sitting upright as before with knees bent and legs crossed, the wine at her lips.

"Oh, how excellent," she exclaimed. "Gabriel has made a fine selection!"

Jesus reclined against the other pillow, raised on one elbow. "May our time together be as wonderful as the wine." He smiled, lowering his chalice and setting it aside. "Please enjoy yours as I share what brings us together."

"It is good I see no wineskin, Jesus"—she smiled—"so that I am limited to one glass. Too much wine can make me babble."

Jesus chuckled. "Well, I'm sure Gabriel could find more if we need it." His eyes scanned the grove and the soft sunlight filtering through the overhead fronds. "He told me you asked for the terebinths. I can see why. It is very pleasant beneath them."

"Yes," she said softly as she surveyed the lush canopy. "My sisters and I often played in the shade of the family grove. Terebinths were the favorite of Eliam, my father. He would begin his day in their quiet as the sun rose. And when the labors of the day were finished, he returned to the grove and found peace as the sun set." She sighed wistfully. "Gabriel's gift reminds me of the joy of the terebinths." She fell silent, reflective, and then continued, "Thank you, Jesus, for allowing me a moment of quiet joy. Now you were about to explain why I am here, weren't you?"

He smiled. "Indeed I was, Bathsheba. During these days in the wilderness, I am seeking a deeper understanding of the influence of the satan on the behavior of man. In the beginning, I Am blessed the heavenly and the earthly beings with the gift of free will—the freedom to make choices—and I Am saw the gift was good, but sometimes choices are made contrary to the good I Am intends." She was listening attentively, her eyes fixed on his. Jesus glanced aside and asked, "Are you aware that David has been here the past couple days?"

Her face registered surprise, though she remained upright and still. "Do you mean the king? King David?"

"Yes," Jesus replied. "King David. Your husband and father of Solomon."

Bathsheba lowered her eyes. A slight shiver raced through her body. "No, I was not aware," she replied pensively. Following a moment of silence, she lifted her eyes and asked, "Why? Why was he here? Did he speak of me?" Her voice was tentative, uneasy. "Is it because of him that you asked for me, Jesus? Have I done something to displease him—or to displease you?"

"No, Bathsheba," he replied softly. "Nothing like that. Your name was mentioned only once in passing as I asked Michael to make arrangements to see you. Only that." He smiled. "You have nothing to fear."

A quiet sigh of relief escaped her. She adjusted the cushion and leaned against it, stretched her legs, and crossed them. "Why David? And if not about me, what did you inquire of him?" She was watching him closely.

His eyes twinkled as he teased, "Are you surprised that you weren't the topic of conversation? A little disappointment, perhaps?"

Sheepishly, she smiled. "Oh, maybe just a little disappointed. I was never really sure of his thoughts of me or the sincerity of his affection. It was not my place. So yes…but maybe more curious than disappointed."

"Well," Jesus continued, "as I mentioned, during these days in the wilderness, I am searching for a deeper understanding of the nature of man and the effect of the satan on a man's behavior. With David, I wanted to explore pride, adulation, and power. Like any man, David had admirable traits. Yet even he fell under the influence of the satan at times—and it seemed that he was especially vulnerable through his pride, through his desire for adulation, and in the misuse of the privilege of power which came with his title as king."

He had her full attention. "There probably has been no better man for probing those things," she reflected. "He certainly craved the adulation and enjoyed the power. So what have you learned?"

"Ah"—Jesus smiled—"you have become the questioner."

"Just curious," Bathsheba giggled, a twinkle in her eyes. "I couldn't help myself. Forgive me."

Jesus took another sip of wine, and she followed suit. His mood turned serious. "I wish to understand *your* behavior, Bathsheba," he continued, taking a second sip. She placed her wine aside and waited. "Do you recall when you first met David—the day while your husband, Uriah, was away at war? Can you describe what happened and how you felt?"

Immediately, she stiffened and sat upright. Her eyes glazed, as though focused far away but not seeing. Slowly, she gathered her thoughts as her eyes shifted to the overhead limbs of the terebinths. "I long tried to forget that day and those moments," she began slowly. "Uriah would often spend time in the palace nearby, plotting strategy with the king. They were close, but I did not know the king. Oh, yes, I would see him from a distance on his favorite black stallion, but he didn't know me. The veils and loose wraps prevented the eyes of men upon me. That was our custom.

"Uriah had left several days before on the next campaign, and the king had stayed behind. Because Uriah was in command over many, his home was lavish with many servants. That day, my hand-maid had prepared a bath for me in the inner courtyard.[21] It was a beautiful day with a cloudless sky. The warmth of the sun matched that of the bath. Only one more moon before my husband would return. That was always the hardest part of the wife of a soldier—the waiting. Always the waiting. So during the bath, I had been thinking of him.

"I had retired to my dressing room wrapped in a towel and was reclining on a lounge. Laisa, my handmaid, was combing my hair—it was much longer then," she reflected and paused. "There was a knock at the door, and Laisa went to answer. There was muffled conversation. When I looked up, two men were standing before me. Laisa had left. 'I sent her away,' the larger man said. 'She is no longer needed. The king has asked for you. Come.' I stood and bowed. After all, they were the king's men, and I, as any subject, would always be available at the call of the king. 'There is no time to prepare', he insisted. 'We must go now.' I grabbed a robe and draped it over my shoulders, the towel wrapped underneath.

"It was my first time in the royal palace with its many doors and hallways. They were in a hurry. It was all very confusing. A magnif-icently carved dark wooden door loomed at the end of a long hall. The smaller man knocked twice, and from within came the com-mand, 'Enter.' He did so, closing the door behind him. There was a brief conversation. The door opened, and the man beckoned me. As I entered, he left and closed the door. Later, I learned they were sentries posted at the door to assure the king's privacy.

"The room was large, tastefully appointed with lounging sofas and chairs. I remember the plush royal-blue carpet. The king was reclining on a sofa with only a loincloth, eyes fixed on me. We were alone. He stood and approached. 'Master,' I said and bowed. He was silent. He removed the robe from my shoulders, then took my hand and led me through an arched doorway to the royal bedroom

---

[21] 2 Samuel 11:2

106

beyond. As we entered, the towel wrap loosened and fell. He lifted me and carried me to the bed." She stopped, tears in her eyes as she turned to Jesus. Sadness had gripped her. "Oh, yes," she continued, "I remember. Do you want more?"

"No," Jesus replied. "No more of those details." Her shoulders sagged with a long slow breath of relief. "We both know how the afternoon ended." With a corner of the soft linen wrap, she dabbed a tear from her cheek. They sat quietly for a few moments. Then Jesus continued, "You have told me what happened. Thank you for your trust. However, I am more interested in your feelings. What were you feeling? Do you recall how you felt from the moment you entered his sitting room until you left?"

Bathsheba shuddered and regained her composure. "You must know something very important to be able to understand my feelings," she began. "It has to do with my husband and my feelings for him. Uriah was a fearless warrior, respected and admired by his men, but he was a kind and tender man to me. Yes, I was always submissive as the culture demanded, but he never treated me that way or took me for granted. In our culture, the concept of love between a husband and his wife was irrelevant. Love had no bearing on the relationship. A wife was the husband's property. A woman was always the lesser of the two in any relationship or interaction.

"Yet I loved Uriah, and he loved me, as any woman knows when she is loved by a man. The love between us was very rare. There are many ways that love is demonstrated by a man toward a woman and by a woman to a man. With Uriah, it was in the soft touch, the tender kiss, the understanding eyes when words were unspoken, and in the yielding to the other in the bedroom.

"When love is present, there is a fullness that is difficult to put into words. Do you understand this, Jesus?" she asked, her eyes moist, her lips quivering with emotion.

Jesus nodded. "I think I do. The bond you shared with Uriah is the oneness that I Am intends and desires."

"So you wish to know about my feelings when entering the king's room and after I left," she reflected, the memories coming back. "Outwardly, the feelings of a woman are of no consequence to a man. And so a girl learns from an early age that feelings are to be kept inside. A woman must always defer to the man—always. So the woman creates and lives within a protective shroud, a shroud outwardly absent of emotion. It is the only way she can survive. The desire of the man is the only thing that matters.

"When the door closed behind me, and I saw the king lying on the sofa with only a loincloth, I knew what was coming. For an instant—a very brief instant—I was flattered that the king would desire me, but then anger. And betrayal. The king had to know my husband was away in battle. In having me, the king had betrayed my husband's loyalty to him—and I felt that betrayal.

"That the king, a man of immense power, could have a woman on impulse with no feeling toward her as a human being made me angry. Yet I couldn't let him see the anger or the betrayal. I was a woman—and he a man. The desire of a man must be satisfied. So I feigned enjoyment, but deep within, the betrayal and the anger seethed and the hatred toward the culture for perpetuating the dominance of men and its unfairness to women. Not just for those moments with the king but for always. That day was a turning point for me. I grew to despise the belittlement of women and the inherent unfairness."

She stopped and her breathing slowed. Jesus had been deeply moved by Bathsheba's story; sadness filled him.

Silence surrounded them. After a few minutes, Bathsheba continued, "I am confused, Jesus." Her eyes were holding his. "As our conversation began, you said something which is contrary to all of my understanding. You said we could talk with each other as equals. 'No master, no servant,' you said, and that we would honor the other in mutual trust without fear. Just a man and a woman, as equals." She paused. "Gabriel had said you are here as a man, and yet you are also the Most High, the Holy of Holies—I Am. Is Gabriel correct?"

Jesus looked at her tenderly. "Gabriel is correct," he replied softly.

"Most respectfully, Jesus, then it is difficult to speak with you as an 'equal.' Yet you have invited me to do so and to place my trust in you." She paused, gathering her thoughts.

"You may do so, Bathsheba. You may speak frankly," Jesus inserted. "What troubles you?"

Her words were measured, respectful. "Why, Jesus?" she asked. "Why must it be so, this disparity between man and woman? You have treated me with tenderness and respect. Why cannot it be so between men and women? Why must the woman always be the lesser and always defer to the whim of the man? Why must it be so?" Her eyes were pleading, overflowing with tears. "Why must women endure belittlement and bear such pain?"

She was not prepared for Jesus's reaction. He was silent, overcome with anguish. Tears filled his eyes as pain overwhelmed him. Tenderly, he peered deeply into her eyes.

"As I Am, that was never my intent or design, Bathsheba," he sighed, a deep sigh which could only be felt by one who has endured disappointment and deep pain. "When the gift of free will is subverted from good to harm, it is the work of the satan who is also exercising free will. It is the dilemma of my greatest gift in creation—the gift of choice between good and evil." He turned silent, reflective. "My desire is to preserve the gift and restore humanity to the beauty I intended.

"Your story underscores my purpose for coming into the world as a man," he said with conviction. "That purpose lies before me." He rose and stretched his hand to lift her. "Thank you for honoring me with your words today, Bathsheba. Your story resonates within me."

Bathsheba bowed deeply. "It has been an honor and privilege, Master," she replied, her eyes returning to his. "May your purpose be fulfilled."

Jesus turned and began retracing his steps to the pool and the shade of the fruit tree. From behind, the yip of the pup brought a smile. Turning, he could see the pup in the distance, bounding toward him across the desert expanse. Gone the terebinth grove, gone Bathsheba.

Gabriel's task was complete.

DAY 19

Jesus
Solitude and Fasting

When with others, the hospitality over shared meals and conversation led to meaningful insights. Solitude, however—away from the distraction of food and person—brought acute understanding. Clarity was essential to the alignment of the human and the divine will. No distractions. And so he had again left before dawn for the distant outcropping.

King David's confession of the insidious nature of adulation and power had surprised him. Not the reality of adulation and power. No, it was the confession. In the confession, Jesus had felt a warm affinity for him—this mighty king, humbly acknowledging the sway of the crowd with its adulation.

In contrast, the intense and intimate pain of Bathsheba because of the lesser status of women filled him with deep sorrow. The anguished eyes and trembling voice remained.

DAY 20

Midmorning
The Satan—Insurrection

The time with David, followed by the conversation with Bathsheba, had drained him. A day to reflect and rest had lifted his spirits. "Storm didn't like that he had no choice," Michael had said. "He isn't used to waiting." Well, it wouldn't be long now. The old oak was not far off. Jesus smiled as he cleared the ridge and began the long descent to the desert floor, partly due to the antics of the ever-present pup, but more so because the vista had changed. No flowing stream this time, no airy canopy, no intimate nesting place, just the gnarled ageless oak.

Sensing a visitor, the pup leapt ahead. Two low stones were arranged under the twisted naked limbs. The midmorning sun cast eerie shadows across them. The satan was seated and leaning against the far one, staring away toward the distant horizon. With the flurry of approaching activity, his head swiveled toward the bounding pup with an empty, icy stare. The pup skidded to a halt and barked defensively. The glare narrowed. With a high yelp, the pup pivoted and sped back to Jesus.

Jesus chuckled at the anxious pup and turned his attention to what lay ahead. Clearly, the intentions of the satan had changed from the earlier visit. What had prompted the satan's brief visit to the pool a couple of days ago and the urgent message to Michael?

Though Jesus's pace had slowed as he approached, the satan showed no signs of impatience. His stare had shifted to Jesus. He continued to lean against the stone—no rising in greeting, no sign of welcome, no invitation to sit. No Delilah this time—she whose eyes had been warm and inviting. No, this time, the satan was as Michael had described: of similar build, with a strong brow and a jaw set in certainty, the open linen shirt, loin wrap, and sandals complementing his natural bronze.

"No Delilah today?" Jesus queried with a smile as he settled against the near stone to face the satan, the pup nestled at his feet. "How unfortunate. It was fun—and oh, so tantalizing." He smirked. "But I suppose it didn't end the way you wanted."

"You had your chance," the satan replied icily. "Whoever or whatever you are, Jesus, you are no ordinary man. Let's just say it ended in a draw and move on."

"Well, I must admit you were a most pleasing host," Jesus replied, "most pleasing." He paused and glanced around. "Clearly this visit is different. Michael was a little put out by your impatience. So what brings us here? And what shall I call you today? Surely not *Delilah*."

"Michael is useless," the satan sneered. "So if he was a little put out, good! It is a mystery to me why he remains in I Aᴍ's good graces. He is useless."

The smile left Jesus's face; the pup eyed the satan warily. "Michael calls you *Storm*," Jesus continued. "Did you know that? *Storm*. And now I'm beginning to see why. You even have the young jackal on edge. So I'll go with that. *Storm* it is."

"Call me whatever you like," the satan said. "I've been called many names, and Storm is as good as any."

"So, Storm, what brings us here?" Jesus repeated. "Why the urgency? Since time is irrelevant to you, what's the rush?"

"A little impatient, are we?" Storm chided. He sat pensively for a moment, and then it came to him—the cold, empty eyes betrayed by a smug smile. "Ah, of course," he continued, "if anyone would be impatient, it would be *you*, Jesus. After all, you are a *man*—a mere mortal. So time works against you." Now there was energy in his voice. "Your time here is limited! Of course. So *you* are the impatient one!" Self-satisfaction had changed his demeanor.

Jesus laughed, and the pup jerked its head at the sound. "You have found my weakness, have you?" He grinned. "My fear of time? It's a most interesting premise, I must admit, and not something I've given any thought to." Jesus chuckled. "Very interesting, indeed," he repeated, scratching behind the pup's ears. "That has nothing to do with why we are here, does it?"

Storm was eager to continue. "Maybe," he replied, "and maybe not. But we can come back to that." His tone and temperament had changed. "You have enlisted the help of Michael—and Gabriel, I see—to bring guests back into my realm. You haven't asked permission, though it hasn't bothered me, but I must confess to being curious.

"Michael tells me that at last count there has been Moses and Elijah, then David, and a couple days ago, Bathsheba. May I assume there will be others? If so, a little notice as common courtesy would be nice. Though I have the power to monitor all in my domain, it is often more entertaining to watch what unfolds from a distance. That seems to be the case here. So I have chosen to let you and Michael play your little games, but sooner or later, I will know all. So then, why this visit, you ask?"

Storm paused, and then continued, "It's quite simple, really. I want to know what you are up to, what you are doing. How long is it going to take, and what do you hope to accomplish? Maybe you don't realize that nothing can be done in this domain without my knowledge or consent. I have extended considerable latitude with you because it intrigues me—and because I always relish the tussles with Michael and his inevitable disappointment in the end." He pushed further, impatience getting the better of him. "Even so, what are you doing?"

"My, you *are* curious." Jesus chuckled and leaned toward the pup, patting its head and back while its tail wagged eagerly. "What do you think, little one? Shall we tell Storm *the plan*?" he asked, stroking the pup and thinking out loud. "That wouldn't be very nice to Michael, would it, pup? To share the plan with Storm but not with him?" He smiled, still talking to the pup. "No, not nice at all." His gaze returned to Storm. "Isn't she adorable? And so understanding." He smiled. "She softens the soul, don't you think? Sort of takes the edge off the day."

"I don't much care for creatures, Jesus," the satan sneered. "And 'softens the soul'? Please. Chattering about *the soul* will get us nowhere. Let's talk about you and why you are here in this place of nothingness." He swept his arm across the landscape. "When we were last together, your mind was not on a lowly dog as I recall. In fact, you seemed to enjoy Delilah. Talk about *softening the soul*," he smirked. "There was a lot of softening going on—at least softening of heart. Desire certainly had its way with you, didn't it—and plea-sure?" he leered. "Ah, how satisfying when a man yields to lust and desire—especially a righteous man. After all, you're a righteous man, aren't you?" The taunt was anything but subtle. "Aren't you, Jesus? Isn't it true that you see yourself as *righteous*—maybe as righteous above all others?" He was enjoying the moment.

The pup had been licking Jesus's hand affectionately as the satan was speaking. Jesus turned to the pup and scratched behind its ears as the pup returned his gaze. "Storm is having fun, isn't he?" he said warmly, the pup wiggling excitedly. "He's toying with me, and I think he's enjoying it." He smiled.

His focus returned to Storm. "Your ways are very effective, I must confess," he began. "In these past few days, I have been seeking to understand how an upright man is led astray. Why does he aban-don the age-old teachings which have shaped him, and above all, why at the very moment when those truths are most needed? Very often, it seems he knows that the choice before him—if the wrong choice—will inevitably lead to harm or suffering." He paused. "So why does he make that choice?"

Storm's eyes had warmed, now riveted on Jesus and eager for more. "Why, indeed?" the satan asked, the smugness returning. "Perhaps the *wrong* choice is not wrong after all. Maybe the *wrong* choice, as you call it, is the *right* choice in that moment. Who is to say what is wrong or right? After all, hasn't man been taught from the beginning he is *created in the image of God*? Aren't then the choices he makes in keeping with that image?" The satan was delighting in the exchange, his sincerity belying its subtle sarcasm. "And if that is true, can *any* choice be wrong? Is not *every* choice right? Is this how you have been spending your precious time, Jesus, pondering right from wrong? Surely there must be something more. Surely you cannot be wasting your time on something so mundane."

Jesus frowned. "What, Storm? Do I sense dismay? Are you disappointed?"

"Surprised," replied the satan, "not disappointed. Why would you waste your precious time on something so insignificant? I was expecting something profound, some grand plan—something beyond human understanding. That is why I wanted to see you, but this?" he sneered. "This is your grand plan?"

Jesus eyed him warily. "The scope of what lies before me is irrelevant to this conversation." His words were controlled, measured. "Is there anything else?"

The satan's countenance changed. He stood, arched his back, and stretched his arms overhead. The pup sprung to its feet, its defenses held in check by a peculiar sense of warmth. "We've been sitting awhile. How about a short walk?" he invited. "The dog might enjoy it, and maybe we'll stumble upon something else to talk about since neither of us is pushed for time," he challenged with a smile. He pointed, and a small shrub appeared. A startled partridge fluttered and skidded low over the ground. The pup lunged, and the chase was on. "You may never see the dog again," the satan chuckled.

"Oh, she always seems to find her way back," Jesus grinned. "She has much to learn though. She chases when there is no possibility of catching. The enthusiasm of youth, I guess." He stood, his eyes on the shrinking pair as the chase led them further away. "Where to? Is there someplace special you have in mind?"

"No, nothing special," Storm replied, walking casually in the pup's tracks. "Just a change of scenery. We've been sitting awhile." It was a pleasant day, with a light breeze and an occasional cloud drifting across the sun.

A casual stroll was a good idea. They walked silently, both absorbing the desert calm. In the distance, the partridge swerved toward a patch of shoulder-high brush where the top branches were tantalizingly beyond the young jackal's reach. "She'll be busy for a while." Jesus smiled. "Surely you must find some delight in animals at play," he said absently as he paused to watch, captivated by their antics.

The satan paused an arm's length away, his eyes on them as well. Jesus was chuckling; the satan was silent, unmoved, expressionless. Slowly he turned, watching Jesus, whose quiet joy baffled him. "Do you have any idea of the extent of my power, Jesus?" he turned serious and asked quietly, an uncharacteristic softness in his voice.

"Some," Jesus replied, eyes fixed on the distant pair. He stood quietly for a moment. "What an odd question. Is there something I should know?"

Storm continued to study him. "Are you impressed, Jesus, with Michael's power? In the middle of this wasteland, he has crafted a refreshing pool in the shade of a marvelous fruit tree, hasn't he? He brings guests at your whim. It seems he has the power to satisfy your every desire, even within the bounds of time. Is that so?" he asked. "Is his power so complete?"

"Michael has all the power he needs," Jesus replied as he resumed the casual stroll, the satan a half pace behind.

Storm had caught up. "Michael has been a witness to my power," he said, "not the fullness of it but enough to respect my command of this realm—this realm within time. My power frustrates him because he knows his power is never enough." He stepped in front, causing Jesus to stop abruptly. "What about you, Jesus? Do you know the extent of my power?" His eyes were leveled on Jesus's.

Jesus returned the gaze. "What do you want from me, Storm?" he asked. "Why were you so anxious to meet?" The satan studied him and then slowly turned to the side.

"I can dance through time," the satan began. "Time doesn't constrain me. It's very handy here." He swept his arm. In an instant, they were in the midst of a small village. "We cannot be seen or heard," he said. "I thought you might enjoy this."

It didn't take long. All was very familiar. They were in Nazareth, the home Jesus had left only a few weeks ago. It was late morning.

The pace of the village was leisurely, peaceful. Here and there, couples were engaged in quiet conversation. A pair of Roman soldiers strolled along the central street, their sandals disturbing the dust with lazy puffs. Villagers watched warily. While soldiers had become a common sight in the past year, there was curiosity. Nazareth was a peaceful village, so their presence had raised suspicions. Muted conversation turned silent as the soldiers approached, then continued after they passed. The soldiers were aloof and kept their distance, seldom engaging with the residents. They were tolerated, not welcome. There was nothing the villagers could do. Rome ruled.

Jesus turned down a side alley, quickened his pace, and followed it toward the village edge. Storm was a step behind, a satisfied smile on his face. In front of a humble dwelling with a trade shop next door, two men were talking. The hair of the older man was long, tied at the back, streaked with gray. His straggly beard hung to his chest, unkempt, more gray than brown. Muscular arms and leathery hands were the marks of his trade: a carpenter. He was shirtless in the morning sun, bent over a well-worn workbench beside the shop door. In his hands, a shaping plane moved carefully back and forth, peeling the roughness from the oak plank clamped to the bench. His keen eyes focused on the grain, avoiding the swirls which grabbed the plane's blade.

The second man was young enough to be his son. Curly brown hair continued around his chin, framing a handsome youthful face. The sand-colored tunic was gathered loosely at the waist with a cord. By the dust on his feet and sandals, it was apparent he had come a distance. He was agitated and waving his hands as he spoke. The older man listened respectfully but remained focused on his work.

"You don't know where he went, and he didn't say when he was coming back?" the young man cried. "It just doesn't make sense. Why would Jesus leave and not tell his father where he was going or how long he'd be gone? And why wouldn't he tell me? We've been friends for over twenty years. It just doesn't make sense." He was exasperated, becoming impatient with the old man. He turned and sat on the stack of planks at the end of the bench, taking a couple of deep breaths to calm himself. "What *did* he say, Joseph? Did he say *anything* that would give a clue?"

The old man set the plane aside and stood upright, stretching his back and flexing his arms and wrists. "I've told you all I know, Caleb," he replied. "What more can I tell you? He said he had to leave, and nothing was going to change that. I talked with him. Mary talked with him. We both talked with him—pleaded with him. All Jesus said was there were things he had to do. He couldn't tell us when he would be back because he said he didn't know. All we do know is that he left here to find his cousin, John. Whatever he had in mind, it was going to start with John." He looked earnestly into the young man's eyes. "And that is all we know. Maybe he didn't tell you because he didn't want to argue with you. He probably knew that you would try to stop him from whatever he had in mind." He sighed—a long, deep sigh. "I just don't know, Caleb. If I did, I would tell you."

Jesus was transfixed. As he listened to Joseph—to the man he admired above all others—he was overcome with sadness. Tears welled in his eyes. Storm too was transfixed—but not on Joseph. He was riveted on Jesus.

Caleb glanced around, making sure no one was nearby. "Listen to me, Joseph," he whispered firmly, grabbing the old man's arm. He bent near, and in a hushed tone, continued, "Does it have anything to do with these damn Romans? I know Jesus bristles at the oppression of our people. Do you think he and John are planning something?" Then it came to him; his eyes widened. "That's it, isn't it! And that's why he doesn't want you or me to know! He doesn't want you to be able to tell anybody anything, and he's protecting me. He doesn't want me to get involved." He turned silent as thoughts ran through his head. "Are you sure you don't know where John is? I've got to find them. They're going to need every man in every village to take on the Romans." He glanced around furtively. "Where do you think John is?"

Joseph grabbed him by the shoulders and shook him, gripping so tightly that Caleb squealed in pain. "Listen to me, Caleb," he admonished. "I don't know where Jesus is, and I don't know where

John is. And I don't know what Jesus is doing. He wouldn't tell me," he said forcefully, glaring at Caleb and still gripping his shoulders. "Do you believe me?"

Caleb squirmed, twisting from Joseph's grip. "Of course, I believe you," he said, his voice still hushed. "Did Jesus say anything about *when*? Do you know the timing of his plan?" Excitement gripped him.

"Caleb, have you been listening to me?" he challenged. "I don't know anything about that. Nothing! The last thing he said in parting was 'I don't know how much time I have.' Now before you go crazy with that, I don't have any idea what that meant. I assume it meant he had to hurry to find John, but I don't know. I just don't know." His eyes had softened. Weariness had overtaken him; his shoulders slumped.

Slowly, Joseph picked up the plane and turned back to the plank. "When you find him, tell him we miss him, and we love him—and he is always welcome home."

As Caleb turned to leave, he looked over his shoulder. "I'll tell him when I see him," he said. "But I'm confident he hasn't forgotten any of those things."

DAY 20

Afternoon
The Satan—Immortality

"I can help you, Jesus," the satan said softly. They were back under the ancient oak where their time together had begun, now resting against the two stones. Nazareth was gone. Jesus had been quiet, deeply moved by the exchange he had witnessed between his father and Caleb. He was troubled; his heart, heavy. The ever-present pup lay curled at his feet.

"Did you hear me, Jesus?" the satan asked quietly. "I can help you. Now that I know a little more, I can help you." He sat patiently. "If only you had told me. It doesn't need to be this difficult. I can help you."

Jesus was somber, his thoughts far away—still in Nazareth. There was nothing he could do about the pain his mother and father were feeling. He had told them all he could. A deep sigh escaped his lips. Slowly his attention returned to the present. He reached and patted the pup, then turned to the satan. "I'm sorry, Storm," he began, "but my thoughts were still in Nazareth. Did you take us there for a reason?"

"Nothing in particular," the satan replied. "Just some fun to demonstrate a little of my power. I thought you might enjoy it. Yet I didn't know what we would see." He paused. "Quite timely for our conversation, don't you think?"

"I've never doubted your power," Jesus replied. "The whole Delilah thing was pretty amazing. That experience got my attention in more ways than you know." He smiled. "It wasn't just the stream or the canopy or pillows or the wine. And just now, stepping across time for a brief visit to home," he reflected, "well, those powers are very impressive, I admit."

The satan was pleased. "There is nothing beyond my power, Jesus." He smiled. "Nothing. And since I now know what is before you, I can help. You can accomplish everything you desire." He paused, one eyebrow raised. "Why have you chosen not to tell me your plan? To do it without my help would be impossible, but with my help—with my power on your side—the Roman legions will cave before you and your armies. It will be the end of their empire, and you will be revered through all time. Tell me more."

Jesus was speechless, staring in disbelief. It was all Jesus could do to keep his emotions under control. He felt bad about the way he had parted from family and friends. But Caleb's outburst, followed by the satan's preposterous theory around this desert sabbatical, had caught Jesus off guard. Suppressing tears of sadness over the partings—and suppressing laughter over the absurdity of the satan's theory—tested his control. He remained stone-faced.

Not so the satan. Energy pulsed through him; he couldn't control his enthusiasm. For centuries after the Greek dynasty, the Romans had been unwitting accomplices to his meddling and oppression of the vast lands and peoples under their control. They had adopted his ways beyond his imagining. They bathed in their arrogance and reveled in their power. Yet he had no loyalty to them—his only loyalty was to himself. Plus he had grown weary of them.

The Roman subjects were clamoring for something new. They were chafing under the strong arm of the imperial state. Even now the pesky Hebrews were turning to anyone making promises to throw off the yoke of Roman oppression. Their putrid pleas for the resurgence of a mighty king, a Messiah, sickened him.

With the brief Nazareth visit, it was becoming clear to the satan as the pieces fell into place. First was Jesus's meeting with Moses, the revered deliverer of the enslaved nation to the Promised Land. Then the huddle with King David, the legendary warrior under whose reign the prowess of the Hebrew armies marched with fear before them. It was, after all, during the reign of David the nation of Israel had dominated the land. That dominance reached its zenith under the glory and wisdom of Solomon, the royal son of King David and Queen Bathsheba. So the visit with Bathsheba was the fine-tuning.

Everything had crystallized. Jesus was putting together a plan to overthrow the Romans and restore the grandeur of the ancient Hebrew nation. Maybe with a little help, this Jesus could *be* that Messiah. Little would they know that the help had come from him or that their savior king would be his pawn. The most beautiful part of all? Jesus, and his dolt Michael, would become *his* loyal subjects. The intrigue gripped him. All that was needed were a couple of empty promises. But it would take all his craftiness to lure the innocent carpenter. He would deal with the dolt later.

"You seem far away, Jesus," the satan began innocently. "We've left Nazareth, you know."

Jesus shook his head to clear it and took a few moments to gather his thoughts. This was bizarre. What was the satan thinking? "I don't understand," Jesus said at last. "Yes, I was reflecting on Caleb's reaction, and you were saying something about helping me. I missed what was in between. What were you saying?"

"I didn't think you were listening, or you would have reacted differently." The satan smiled. "I said that I could help you. Now that I know your plan, I can help."

Jesus parried. "What is my plan…and how can you help?"

The satan chuckled. "You are a cagey one." He smiled. "I like that." He was warm, engaging, friendly. "Caleb was right. You are planning to overthrow the Romans and lead your people to liberty and freedom——a noble ambition. I can help."

Jesus was enjoying this. "How can you help?" he asked innocently. "Do you have any idea how many men that would take? There aren't enough in all Israel to counter the Roman army. Do you have legion upon legion of mercenaries at your disposal? If you do, where are they?"

"Ah, you're interested." The satan grinned. "Think—overwhelming odds in your favor, weapons of destruction the invincible Romans have never seen, centurions abandoning Caesar, city after city cowering before you, pleading for mercy at the whisper of your coming. Terror and fear in every corner, all across the empire." The satan stood. "You would rule the world," he declared, sweeping his arms broadly.

Jesus rose to his feet. "How would you do this? And what do you want in return?"

"There's more, Jesus." The satan was pleased with himself and with Jesus's questions. "The *how* is irrelevant. Armies, destruction, war—all are within my power. But for you—only for you—something more, something I have never given to any of my followers. Only for you."

"You have my attention, Storm," Jesus said calmly. "What do you have that would be so important to me after I have conquered the world?"

The satan stood before him, peering deeply into his eyes. "Release from time, Jesus. Never have I released a mortal from the chains of time. You would be the first. No death. No concern over whether you will have enough time. For you, time would be no more. You would join me in ruling the earthly realm—never giving another thought to time. Step in and out as you please. After you have conquered the world, you decide who thrives and who doesn't. Together, we reshape the world. You wield the power."

"What's the catch," Jesus said. "If I agree, what's the catch? Where are you in all of this?"

"We would be equals, Jesus, you and I. Partners together, reshaping the world." The satan held out his hand. "Take my hand and let it begin. It begins from this moment."

Jesus peered deep into his eyes. The satan didn't flinch. "What about Michael?" Jesus deflected. "Is there a place for Michael in this?"

"Of course there would be a place for him, Jesus, a highly elevated, crucial role," he said, his eyes darting excitedly. "Don't worry about Michael. I'll speak with him. He will be taken care of as your loyal confederate."

"Even so," Jesus said coyly, "I'd like to speak with Michael before responding to this magnanimous proposal. He has been very faithful to me. When do you need to have my answer?"

"Go ahead, talk with Michael. Take as long as you like, Jesus, any time before you depart your sabbatical." The satan dropped his hand. "Just remember, once you decide, there is no *when*. *When* is a matter of time, and from that instant, you would be free of time."

The satan turned and was gone.

As Jesus began to retrace his steps to the pool, the young pup sped ahead. Jesus smiled.

"What a day," he said to himself. "What a day!"

DAY 21

Rest

On the seventh day, he rested.

DAY 22

Elijah
Free Will

The bed of leaves brought warmth and comfort through the night. He had slept soundly. Somewhere from afar, the undulating tones of a lone nightjar roused him in the early-morning light. Slowly, Elijah rubbed his eyes and lay still, reveling in the haunt of the distant call. He was grateful Michael had arranged for him to return at dusk yesterday to help adjust to the effects of time. Slumber had come easily following the quiet, lighthearted conversation with Jesus and him—and the wine.

Propped up on his elbows, in the dim light he could see he was alone. He sat upright.

Odd. Very odd. "Where have they gone," he wondered aloud, "and what lies ahead?" There was no sign of them, no trail in the desert sand, emptiness but for the oasis surrounding him.

He rose and waded into the cool spring water, refreshed by the chill. Near the tree trunk on a flat stone lay a loaf of bread, some cheese, and fruit. *Thank you, I Am,* he prayed. The bread was warm, the cheese cool, the fruit lush. He ate leisurely, all the while wondering where Jesus and Michael were and why he had been left alone.

The soft rustle in the leaf-laden branches from the gentle breeze was soothing. The shade and the cool water were peaceful. Elijah lay back on the bed and watched the leaves sway gently in the breeze. He slept.

Time was no longer a constraint. The widow's son was sharing how their life had changed, as though given new life through the miracle of the oil and flour. [22] The raven soared overhead in ever-widening circles.[23] And now Elisha was tugging his tunic from behind. "What is it, my friend?" he asked as he turned, but Elisha was not there. There was nothing there. Yet again, the tug on his tunic…and again. "What? Who?"

Now roused awake, Elijah rolled. Surprised, the mischievous lion cub let go of the tunic and jumped back. "What…?" struggled Elijah, shaking off sleep. "What is going on?" Playfully, the cub leapt forward and caught the tunic again. It was a game.

"He found his prey, I see," the voice chuckled. Elijah turned to find Jesus approaching, a broad smile on his face. "He's been on the prowl ever since we left. Michael lured him with bread scraps, but when they ran out he left us, looking for more. I guess he couldn't resist the gold sash and fancy silk tunic." Jesus grinned. "Neither could Moses the last time you were here as I recall."

Elijah stood, and they embraced. "Last night was fun," Elijah said, "but I guess I wasn't very good company. The last I remember, Michael was beginning to tell about David's visit and the fun he and Gabriel had with that. I didn't catch very much of it. Must have been the wine…"

Jesus laughed. "Well, I'm sure Michael won't mind repeating it. They enjoyed themselves with that assignment. And I must confess he knows how to tell a story!"

"Where is Michael?" Elijah asked. "Is everything okay?"

"Oh yes," Jesus replied, "he's fine. He's off on another assignment. I like to keep him on his toes!"

"Well, judging from last night, you're doing that quite well." Elijah smiled. "He still seems a little perplexed about your time here." He paused and studied Jesus. "How can I be of help to you, Jesus? Before parting last time, I recall Moses saying you were exploring

---

[22] 1 Kings 17:8–16
[23] 1 Kings 17:3–6

the nature of doubt. He said your questions were painful—in fact, 'excruciating,' to use his words."

"Yes, I felt bad my questions caused so much pain for him," Jesus said. "That wasn't my intent, but his experience in dealing with doubt was very helpful."

"How so?" Elijah asked attentively.

Jesus smiled. "With Moses and with others, I have been seeking a deeper understanding of the consequence of the gift of *free will*—and sadly, when choices lead to hurt or harm. Because you lived in the earthly realm, you perhaps experienced such consequences, whether the result of a choice you made or of a choice made by others."

Elijah studied him. "Interesting, Jesus. Very interesting," he pondered, then slowly continued, "I don't think it is possible for a human to live in this realm without those experiences, for good or bad. Seems to me just *living* is a never-ending series of choices. And every choice has a consequence.

"When life is going smoothly, the choices flow smoothly, and their consequences flow seamlessly as well. Yet with one bad choice, life can pivot, and the consequences send it into a downward spiral of hardship and suffering. I observed people living those lives many times and experienced some of that myself. Sometimes those choices are made without thinking, the result of poor habits. Often, the more severe consequences are the result of a conscious choice. Eventually the pain and suffering can be followed by feelings of emptiness and regret, and hope is lost.

"On the other hand, there are those who navigate life with more joy than sorrow or joy in the face of sorrow. They have somehow learned to resist the urge of the wrong choice. Some of that, I suppose, is having learned from past mistakes. But some also seems to come from a deepened understanding of God's intent with the gift—an intent for good, not harm, of purpose and of hope.

"I apologize, Jesus." Elijah paused with a smile. "Here I am rattling on, boring you to tears."

"Not in the least, Elijah." Jesus chuckled. "You have sensed well my struggle these days. Your insights and experience with this gift are very helpful. Don't stop," he encouraged.

Elijah sat quietly, enjoying the serenity—the gentle midday breeze, the soft rustle of the overhead leaves, the subtle rippling of the pond. "This is quite a place Michael and the heavenly hosts prepared for you, Jesus, in the middle of the wilderness," he reflected. "Was it their intent, do you suppose, to remind you that in the midst of your wilderness journey, whether in these days or in whatever your future holds as a man, there is always a place to return for comfort and encouragement? I wonder…" Jesus remained silent, focused intently on Elijah. "Michael has shared a little of what has been going on," Elijah continued. "He has been trying to figure things out, but I sense some frustration in his lack of understanding. Not that he doubts, Jesus. No, not that. Yet I sense genuine confusion as he seeks to please you in serving."

"At the right time, Elijah, he will understand all," Jesus said quietly. "At the right time."

"Michael's devotion to you is unwavering. Surely you know that," Elijah replied.

"Never in doubt." Jesus smiled. They sat quietly, the pleasant day surrounding them, unhurried.

Interrupting the reverie, Elijah continued, "Michael said something that intrigues me. Some of his assignments have taken him to the satan—*Storm*, he prefers to call him." He smiled. "In a quiet moment, Michael said he believes Storm's sole purpose is *to wound the heart of God*. Has he shared that with you?"

"Yes," Jesus replied, "he has."

"Well, if that is so," Elijah reflected, "where better to enter the depth of God's heart than through humanity—and how most certain to wound that heart than by subverting the gift of free will?"

DAY 23

Elijah
Power of the Spirit

The evening and morning had passed leisurely. Now the mid-day dip in the pool stimulated further conversation around the consequences of human choice. They were resting in the shade of the tree, Jesus sitting with his back against its trunk, while Elijah lay on the bed of leaves. The lion cub had found its way back to Elijah, who enjoyed teasing it with an occasional toss of bread scraps. The cub's antics delighted them. When the bread ran out, so did the cub as it ambled off.

"Your insights have been helpful, Elijah," Jesus reflected, "but I asked for your return for a different purpose. The conversation around free will has been an unexpected blessing, and I am grateful for it."

"I wondered," Elijah replied, "though it has been an interesting topic to explore." He paused. "So how can I be of help?"

"I am intrigued about the last moments of your life," Jesus began. "First, about Elisha's request for twice the power of your spirit, and second, that you didn't die.[24] You have long been revered as the greatest of prophets, Elijah. The stories of your mighty powers and the fiery chariot and whirlwind which carried you to heaven have been told and retold through countless generations."

---

[24] 2 Kings 2:1–14

"So in all your thirty years of living within time, those things have intrigued you?" Elijah chuckled. "Surely there must be plenty of things in life which would be far more fascinating to a young man than old stories told by old men!"

"Well, when you put it that way," Jesus laughed. "There are a few other things to pique a man's interest, I confess."

"And what might some of those be, Jesus?" Elijah asked, a twinkle in his eye. "You can trust me. Who am I going to tell?" he teased.

"Moses told me you liked to tease," Jesus nodded with a smile. "I guess I'll need to be wary—and I thought it was just the satan I had to worry about." Elijah snickered. "Yet"—Jesus's tone and countenance were turning serious—"I want to explore the nature of the extraordinary power of the Spirit which was at work within you. When did you know you had received that power? And how did you decide when to use it?" He was staring intently at Elijah.

Elijah stood and stretched, his gaze turned into the distance. He was thinking, remembering. He turned toward Jesus and sat down on the bed of leaves, studying them as he pondered Jesus's question. Slowly he lifted his head to engage Jesus's stare. "I'm not sure when I first realized the power which God had given me," he began. "The first time I remember was during a famine when the widow and her son and household had only a meager amount of flour and oil— enough for their last meal. The Spirit power brought flour and oil in abundance, and it seemed that from then, on the Spirit was ever present.

"How did I decide to use that power? A very interesting question. The power seemed to flow when God willed it. I was just the instrument God used. I'm sure many people thought I had some miraculous powers, but the power was never mine. It was God's power—and God always seemed to use it to make a point or to serve a larger purpose."

"Why did God choose you, Elijah?" Jesus asked. "And what do you think was the larger purpose God had in mind when the power was released through you?" His gaze was unwavering, intently focused on Elijah.

Elijah reached for a handful of leaves and absently tossed them, watching them settle softly on the ground. "I don't know why God chose me. There were plenty of times I asked myself that question and wished God had picked someone else," he reflected. "Yet it seems to me God always does the choosing—we don't get to choose. And when God chooses, sooner or later, God's will takes over. When that happens, the power flows and attitudes and hearts are changed. And maybe that is God's larger purpose: that when people experience or witness the power of the Spirit, hearts and attitudes are changed. For some perhaps, the result is a course correction in their lives. For others—those *stiff-necked* ones, as Moses called them—change does not come, and their lives continue as before, and pain and suffering deepens. Maybe that's what God had in mind, Jesus." He paused. "I don't know. The mystery of God was beyond my understanding. What I *do* know is that when God wanted to make a point, the power flowed. And it always got people's attention!" He turned to Jesus. "I'm not sure this is very helpful, Jesus. What are you thinking?"

Jesus sat quietly, studying the sand beneath him at the foot of the tree. He gathered a handful and brought it close, studying it absently, slowly letting it drizzle through his fingers. Then another handful, and then another. He lifted his eyes to the far horizon, as though he were looking across time.

Slowly, his eyes focused as his thoughts crystallized. "Yes, it seems that across the generations, I Am has breathed the power of the Spirit into and through the prophets for each day and time, whether stiff-necked or not, though it seems very little has changed in the nature of man—from the first generation through all generations. Even when the power of the Spirit was doubled—as with your student, Elisha—the nature of man wasn't changed over time. The old ways always seem to return."

He had Elijah's complete attention. "It came to me in the sand," Jesus said, reaching for another handful. He swept the other hand and his eyes across the desert plain. "The power of the Spirit is limitless, more plentiful than the grains of sand in this desert." His gaze returned to study the sand cradled in his fingers. Elijah was fixated on the handful of sand. "Your story has indeed been very helpful,

Elijah," he continued. Very slightly, he cracked apart the middle fingers. Almost imperceptibly, a near-invisible sheet of sand began to trickle to the ground. "The power of the Spirit released through the prophets has been like this sand. Yes, it is power filled. Across time up to now, it has been released through a very few in each generation."

He slowly opened the cracks between the other fingers, and the trickle of sand grew. With handful after handful, he opened the cracks as though releasing more and more of the power of the Spirit.

"What if the power of the Spirit were released in each generation through many—not just a few—and those who receive the Spirit have the power to reach across all of humanity, not just the few within earshot of a lone prophet? If the power of the Spirit were released in greater measure, might the will of the satan be held in check, and might the trajectory of humanity be altered? That's what I was thinking, Elijah." He reached for another handful of sand. "What if the power of the Spirit were released through many, not just a few." Another handful, and then another.

Elijah watched the sand as it trickled through Jesus's fingers. "Fascinating," Elijah remarked, "a vision of promise and hope." He paused, reflecting, and then continued, "We both know that the satan is very resourceful, far more resourceful than man. And he is pretty pleased with the state of humanity. So as the power of the Spirit is given to more and more people, how will they know the intent of God when they receive that power? What if because of the satan's power, they each decide the power given to them is to be used according to *their* sense of God's will, aligned with *their* way of thinking—and the will of God is not at its center? A bunch of power-filled zealots, each determined to go their own way, would be of no more value in changing the human trajectory than before. After all, the influence of the satan never ends—even to the point of death."

Jesus smiled. "More for me to ponder, Elijah. I can see why you are revered among the prophets!"

DAY 24

Elijah
Death

The midday stroll had taken them over the far ridge where Jesus had nodded toward the ancient oak at the valley floor. Elijah delighted in Jesus's memories of the visits with the satan, and especially about Delilah. "She had your full attention, did she?" he smirked. "You're a little coy around its ending. Isn't there more to tell? Or am I going to have to rely on Michael to fill in the blanks?"

"Well, good luck with that," Jesus laughed. "Michael found me the next morning at the foot of the tree, sound asleep. He peppered me with questions all the way back until I told him it was a memorable evening, and that was the way I intended to leave it. After that, he quit asking." He smiled. "So he's still trying to figure out these visits with the satan, but at the right time, he will know."

"Poor Michael," Elijah sighed. "Surely, you must test his patience."

"Yes, I suppose I do," Jesus reflected, staring at the distant tree. He stood quietly, deep in thought, and then turned about. "Let's head back. I'm sure Michael will have returned by now, so no sense having him in a stew again." He chuckled.

Elijah turned the tables on the way back, delighting Jesus with memories and tales of the power of the Spirit. As they neared the oasis, the robed one stood and waved in greeting, and immediately, the lion cub and the jackal pup dashed toward them, tumbling over each other along the way as each tried to outrun the other. Laughter filled the air.

"Well," Jesus chuckled, "it looks like Michael found your friend!"

"No," Elijah rejoined, "more likely, my friend found Michael!"

*****

After rinsing his hair and beard and washing the dust from his feet, Elijah was sitting at the base of the tree. Jesus and Michael were reclined near the pool, within easy reach of the platter of fresh fruit and cheese Michael had prepared.

"Once again, Michael"—Elijah smiled, raising a goblet of wine—"you have selected well." Michael beamed. "Where have you been all day? We've missed you."

Michael took a sip and nodded toward the ridge over which they had come. "I was going to go survey that old oak in the far valley," he began, "but not long after setting out, the cub and the pup caught up with me and headed off a different direction. So I followed them, enjoying their antics." He turned back to Elijah. "I dare say I have had an easier couple days than you. No doubt Jesus has been peppering you with questions." He smiled, glancing at Jesus.

Jesus chuckled. "Well, I can't speak for Elijah, but I have been enlightened by our conversations," he said, raising his goblet. "And indeed, the wine is excellent. Thank you, Michael."

"Of course." Michael smiled. He lifted the platter, passed it to Jesus and then to Elijah. "The cheese complements the fruit, don't you think?" Lighthearted conversation flowed as fruit, cheese, and wine were enjoyed. No one seemed to be in a hurry, which added to Michael's frustration. "So now what?" he asked impatiently, watching Jesus. "What's next?"

"I see what you mean, Jesus," Elijah chuckled, nodding toward Michael. "He *does* seem a little impatient." He turned to Jesus. "Give him a break. How about a little insight so he has some idea of what lies ahead? Just a little." He prodded Jesus playfully.

Jesus grinned. "Moses had you pegged, Elijah. You do like to tease." He turned toward the pool, studying the pup and cub nestled on the far side, at rest after their long day. "Here's what's next, Michael," he said, studying the distant pair. "Actually, I'm glad you returned. There is one more thing I want to explore with Elijah today, and your thoughts will be helpful too. Tomorrow and the day after will again be solitude for me. The next day, I'd like to talk with Hagar, Abraham and Sarah's servant, so that is your next assignment. While I'm away and with Hagar, it would be a good time for you to meet again with Storm under the old oak. He has something to talk with you about, and I have a feeling you will be surprised at how pleasant he can be."

Elijah watched Michael closely, anticipating with delight his reaction. "Sounds like fun, Michael." He grinned.

Michael was fixed on Jesus, ignoring Elijah. "*Storm?* You want me to meet with *Storm?*" he exclaimed, his eyes bulging. "Jesus, you know how much I despise him, and you know he despises me even more. Why do you want me to do this? Nothing good can possibly come of it, so why do it?" His voice trembled, the agitation creasing his brow where beads of sweat had gathered. He rose, strode several paces along the pool's edge, and dropped his cloak to cool off. He turned to Jesus. "Spare me this, Jesus, I beg you!" he cried and sank to his knees.

Jesus reached for the platter, rose, and walked to Michael's side. Kneeling, he said softly, "Michael, my beloved, relax. Have some fruit and cheese. And relax." He sat beside him. "No harm will come to you. You know that because you know me." He paused. "Now come, we have a guest." He smiled and glanced toward Elijah.

Michael sighed—a long, deep sigh—and reached for the fruit and cheese, nibbling each slowly. "You're right," he said, looking at Jesus. "We do have a guest. I'm sorry." He smiled, glancing toward Elijah. "And of course, I will do your bidding and meet with Storm. And of course, I trust you. If, as you say, it proves to be a pleasant visit, well, that would be a first," he chuckled. "Maybe he will shed some light on your meetings with him." He smiled. "Storm has a way of getting under my skin, so we will see what he has to say." He paused. "And Hagar? That will be a pleasure. Needless to say, once again, I am curious."

Jesus smiled, then rose and returned with the platter to Elijah, offering him more cheese and fruit. Michael returned as well, and lighthearted conversation continued.

"So what is the *one more thing*, Jesus?" Michael asked. "What more are you seeking from Elijah?"

Elijah grinned. "He wants to know why I didn't die, Michael," he chuckled. "At least, I think that is the *one more thing*. Am I right?" He looked to Jesus, raising his glass. Michael turned to Jesus, perplexed.

"Right you are," acknowledged Jesus. "Scripture and tradition teaches that you 'ascended in a whirlwind into heaven'[25] as Elisha watched. Why? Why did you not die?"

"I believe it was the will of God," Elijah replied. "There is no other explanation. Is that not so?"

Jesus looked to Michael, then back to Elijah. "But why?" Jesus asked. "Why would it be the will of God that you not experience death? Yes, you were a mighty prophet, but all the other great prophets died—even Moses. Why do you think God chose to deliver you from the sting of death?"

Elijah sat silently. "I do not know the mind of God," he replied softly. He was confused. Michael had explained he would be interacting with I Am in the man, Jesus. Yet here was Jesus—I Am—seemingly uncertain of what may lay ahead.

Jesus turned to Michael, his face forlorn. "What do you think, Michael?" he asked, his eyes sorrowful. "You have served I Am since the beginning. Why do you think I Am chose to free Elijah from the sting of death?"

Michael was beginning to understand. It was the man, Jesus, before him—not I Am. Michael was beginning to understand that at times, Jesus's humanity would bring doubt, uncertainty, even fear. That was the reason for the visits with Moses, with David, and now with Elijah. Jesus the man was trying to understand and anticipate what the future would bring and to learn from their experiences—

---

[25] 2 Kings 2:11

hoping to avoid their pitfalls. Here, the man Jesus was confronting the inevitability of what would eventually befall even him: death. Unless perhaps by learning from Elijah, he could find another way. After all, Elijah didn't die. And he knew he was greater than Elijah—so death could be avoided.

Jesus was staring at Michael while the question hung in the air: *Why do you think I AM chose to free Elijah from the sting of death?* His mind had wandered to the recent episode with the satan. Truth be told, the immortality proposed by Storm intrigued him. Perhaps the satan was on to something: one immortal engaging across each generation, generation after generation through all of time. Truths spoken and taught by that person consistent across every generation could, indeed, reshape humanity.

Michael's response brought him back to the moment. "Does scripture give a clue, Jesus?" Michael asked, imploring the man, Jesus. "You know the rabbinical texts. What do they say about why Elijah was spared the sting of death?"

Jesus stood, slowly shifting his weight from side to side in a rhythmic sway. He studied Elijah who was sitting silently, observing this man standing before him. Jesus turned to Michael and then slowly back to Elijah. "You had told Elisha if he saw you being taken into heaven, then he would know that his request for double your power would have been granted. If not, his request would be denied. Fifty prophets had followed Elisha and were standing across the Jordan, watching but unable to hear." He paused. "Do you remember?"

"Like it was yesterday," Elijah answered.

"We know what happened," Jesus continued. "You ascended, and I AM *did* grant the double portion of power to Elisha—and those nearby eventually became witnesses to that power." Jesus sat, staring across the pool in the distance, deep in thought. The eyes of Michael and Elijah were fixed on him.

Slowly, Jesus turned to them. The answer had come to him. "Escaping death wasn't the point," he reflected, "'double the portion of your spirit' was. I AM used the whirlwind and your ascension as the sign of I AM's power to apportion the Spirit in answer to prayer.

Elisha's request was a prayer, and you knew that, a prayer only God could answer."

He turned silent. For the past few days, he had been unable to shake the words of the satan: "Never have I released a mortal from the chains of time. You would be the first. No death. No concern over whether you will have enough time. For you, time would be no more." Now the possibility of also avoiding the pain of death gripped him. Elijah, sitting before him, was proof of *that* possibility too.

He had come into time to change the trajectory of humanity. Might there be a way to accomplish both—to affect the change his heart desired *and* avoid the finality of dying? Elijah didn't die, and his follower, Elisha, received twice the power.

Yet even with double the power, Elisha's time had no lasting effect in offsetting the power of the satan. It remained unabated and the trajectory of humanity unaltered. Doubling the power of the Spirit in one man had affected humanity for only a brief moment in human history: the moment of that man's life. Yes, acts of power in that moment were impressive to be sure—as the life of Elijah, and then of Elisha, were testament to—but the human trajectory beyond their lifetimes was unchanged.

Something was missing. *Did the answer lie in the satan's offer*, he wondered—to remain within time without dying and span the generations in order to shift the trajectory? After all, Elijah had left. The mantle of power had been shifted to Elisha's shoulders. Yet even Elisha eventually left, and gradually, the people fell back into the old patterns of the satan.

"Okay, Elijah," Jesus began, turning toward him, "let's follow your thinking that it was God's will that you not die. That would, of course, have to be so, but what if you simply had disappeared for a time? What if Elisha's followers had, in fact, found you three days later in the hills? What if you never died and had instead remained within mankind for the rest of time?" His eyes returned to absently study the cub and pup on the far side of the pool. "What if you were to retain the Spirit power you had been given *and* were freed to proclaim the love of God in each generation—you, as God's great messenger, generation after generation? How might humanity be different today if that had been the plan?"

"But that didn't happen, Jesus," Michael inserted. "If we follow Elijah's thought, that clearly *wasn't* the plan. So why waste time wondering about it?" He was exasperated. "It didn't happen. End of story. So once again, what are we doing, and why are we here?"

"Ah, my friend," Jesus replied, turning to him. "you are so very faithful and earnest in your trust." He paused and turned back to Elijah. "What are your thoughts? Why did you leave and not come back? And how would things have changed if you had?"

Elijah was fascinated—both in Jesus's ponderings and Michael's anxiety. "I don't have answers to your questions, Jesus," he admitted softly. "I simply don't know what was in the mind of God then or now, but maybe it had nothing to do with not dying. Maybe it was about the power of the Spirit and to whom that power was given. Maybe the answer rests there and not in the dying." He paused. "I don't have answers."

Jesus's eyes narrowed and shifted to the sand beneath him, his brow furrowed, deep in thought. Slowly he repeated, "'Maybe it had nothing to do with not dying. Maybe it was about the power of the Spirit and to whom that power was given.'"

His eyes lifted, first to Elijah, then to Michael and back to Elijah. "Maybe so," he said, "maybe so."

DAY 25, 26

Jesus
Solitude and Fasting

I AM in the man Jesus, both divine and human, had been intrigued with the recent interactions—with the satan and his offer of immortality, and with Elijah to further explore free will, to ponder the manifestation of the Spirit in the world, and to contemplate the reality and mystery of death. A time apart with no distractions was key. Only water to quench thirst: the ever-present reminder of Jesus's humanity.

DAY 27

Hagar
Rejection

"She asked only for bread and water," Michael said, "and some shade among the boulders." He pointed. The distant outcroppings interrupted the flat barren wilderness. It was where the jackal pup had first found Jesus.

"Well, good things have come from those rocks." He smiled. "Come, pup," he called, "let's go home!" The pup jumped with excitement at the sound of the clapped hands. Michael watched as the man and pup set out, the pup darting here and there while Jesus's laughter faded away.

They'll be a while, Michael thought. He strolled to the bed of leaves and stretched out. *A nap always refreshes.* He smiled. *Any time of day.*

*****

"In the early years, they were kind to me," her story began. "I don't remember how it was I came to be a slave of Abram, or why I was picked to serve his wife, Sarai.[26] Yet in time, Sarai and I became very close. And as I said, in the early years, they were kind to me."

---

[26] Genesis 16:1–16

Hagar delighted to learn Jesus had come among these crags early one morning to pray and of the persistent young jackal who had tugged irreverently at his tunic. She laughed as Jesus's eyes twinkled in telling the story, especially when he lifted the frayed hem of the tunic and playfully scolded the pup. Now the pup was focused on the visitor and had settled at her feet, enjoying the gentle strokes along its side and down its back.

She listened attentively as Jesus related experiences of recent days—especially Bathsheba's memories—and the tenderness in his telling, occasionally pausing to enjoy the cool water and fresh bread. She was beginning to understand why Michael had intimated she would find the time with Jesus to be a time of comfort and sincerity.

They were sitting on shallow stone benches in the shade of the outcropping. She was enjoying the memories of midmorning breezes as one gently swept occasional strands of hair across her face. Long black tresses complemented the richness of her ebony skin; black lashes framed the deep-brown eyes, reminders of her Egyptian lineage. A single woven chord of silver hung loosely around her neck, stopping just short of the V in the soft apricot cotton wrap. Her presence and beauty were subdued, as of a woman with inner strength accustomed to serving faithfully at the pleasure of others.

"Tell me what you remember about life with Abram and Sarai," Jesus had asked.

"Well, as I said Sarai and I became very close, so she often confided in me more than with the other servants." Hagar began. "As the years passed, Sarai and Abram tried again and again to conceive, but nothing came of it. In time, she began to worry that childbearing had passed her by, and Abram would never have a son—an heir. One day, we walked to the spring for water together, which was unusual because that was my job, and she never accompanied us to the pool, so something seemed odd. I had just filled my jars and was lifting them to my shoulders when she stopped me and directed me to sit with her and rest for a bit.

"Sarai's eyes were tear-filled. She was downcast. Whatever had been bothering her the last few days had reached its low ebb. She turned to me and shared her solution to the problem. Because I was much younger, she knew I could bear children, though I had never slept with a man. So since I was her favored slave, she was going to offer me to Abram as a wife so I could bear him a child, and he would have his heir. It was Sarai's nature—very giving and unselfish. Her concern was for her husband and providing an heir."

Jesus recalled this part of the Abrahamic legacy as preserved in the Torah, yet the sacred scrolls offered little detail. "What was Abram's reaction," he asked, "when Sarai suggested her idea? Were you there?"

"No," Hagar replied. "At Sarai's instruction, we had prepared Abram's favorite meal with a new skin of wine. Once the meal began, we were dismissed. They dined longer than usual, with quiet conversation until the fire died. When we were called to clear things away, Sarai took me aside and told me of the plan. I would become Abram's wife after seven days of preparation.

"Those days flew by, and I was very nervous. Abram watched me closely during those days, with tender smiles but few words. Soon the entire clan knew Abram was taking a second wife. That night, my shyness with him was no more.

"Abram's tenderness toward Sarai and toward me never changed. He was very kind to her, and to me. Even though I bore him a son, Ishmael, everyone understood Sarai was his first wife—and I, his second. He saw Ishmael and me as the gift of Sarai's unselfish sacrifice. His love for Sarai, Ishmael, and me was never in doubt. He was an amazing man and wonderful father. In his eyes, I was no longer a slave. With marriage and especially with Ishmael, I had become 'family.'"

"So Ishmael grew past weaning and through boyhood," Jesus recalled. "What was it like in those years? How did your treatment by Sarai and Abram change?"

"Those bonds only deepened." She smiled quietly. "In some ways, Sarai almost saw Ishmael as her own. She was very proud of him. At the wedding night, I had become accepted. As Ishmael grew, I felt favored by Abram in the same way he favored Sarai as his first wife. So I had moved from *property* as a slave girl to being *accepted* as part of the family, to *favored* as the mother of the heir—all with the blessing of Sarai. Those were magical years for Ishmael and me." The smile began to fade, and she fell silent.

Jesus rose and petted the pup at her feet. The pup stretched, its tail wagging as it licked the back of his hand. "May I sit here?" he asked, nodding to the empty space on her stone an arm's length away.

"Please." She smiled shyly, waving her hand. They paused, both enjoying the gentle breeze. The water and bread refreshed, and the pup entertained them as it pounced on bits of tossed bread. Subdued laughter filled the air, and then quiet returned.

Slowly, Jesus began. "Then things changed with the miracle of Sarai's pregnancy." He tilted his head, his eyes engaging hers. "What was that like?"

Hagar turned and stared across the desert floor. "You know, Abram would boast when traders came by. He would point to Ishmael as he played and beam, 'How many men do you know who father a son after eighty-six years?' They would laugh and embrace him, shaking his hand in envy and glee. He loved to brag about his son and about Sarai's gift of me—and they would look at me, nod, and smile respectfully. And as I said, Abram was a good man. He was proud of Ishmael and doted over him as only a father could."

She stood, slowly stepping across the shadow into the sunlight and continuing to stare across the desert. "When Ishmael was thirteen, something odd happened. Abram said he was visited by God. He changed his name to Abraham, and he changed Sarai's name to Sarah. And he had the foreskins of all the males in the clan cut away, including Ishmael's.[27] I remember that day vividly because Ishmael wanted to please his father and not cry like the younger boys, but when it was just him and me, he cried—and I held him. He wanted so badly to please his father. Abraham never knew Ishmael cried."

Hagar turned toward Jesus, her dark hair glistening in the sun. "About a year later," she continued, "three men visited.[28] I remember the feast that was prepared and Sarah and I making bread for them. Sarah told me later they told Abraham that she would conceive and

---

[27] Genesis 17:23–27
[28] Genesis 18:1–15

bear his son. 'Abraham laughed,' she said, and so did she when she told me. Here they were, almost a hundred years old! And I laughed too because it was so absurd.

"Yet a few months later, when Sarah announced she was pregnant—well, we were shocked and elated. Of course, Abraham glowed with pride, after all, he was one hundred years old and going to be a father again! We were all so very jubilant. A few months later, when Isaac was born, it seemed like the whole world celebrated. Joy was everywhere. His birth was indeed a miracle. He was proof of God's promise to Abraham."

She slowly walked to the other bench and sat alone. She stared at the pup, again lying at her feet.

Jesus shifted, watching her closely. "But things changed," he said softly. The story was well-known, having been told through the generations, including thousands of years later in the synagogue in Nazareth and in his home.

"Oh, how things changed," she sighed, stroking the pup. "Ishmael loved his little brother. And Abraham delighted in watching them play. It was when Isaac was weaned—old enough to leave his mother's breast—that things changed quickly.[29] Sarah became very cold to me and very sharp and dismissive of Ishmael. It wasn't that Ishmael misbehaved or did anything wrong—nothing like that. He was a good son and loving brother. I couldn't put my finger on it, but she had changed—or at least her attitude toward Ishmael and me changed. You could see it in her eyes. She no longer confided in me—in fact, she shunned me—and she despised Ishmael. No matter how hard Ishmael and I tried, we were unable to satisfy her. It was baffling. He was only fifteen and had done nothing to deserve it, but she no longer wanted him in her sight and certainly no longer near Isaac. Isaac would cry because he loved his brother and wanted to play with him. They had grown so close. It didn't make any difference. Abraham's love for Ishmael and for me continued to deepen, while Sarah's heart had hardened for reasons I could not understand."

---

[29] Genesis 21:8–19

Hagar stopped and turned her eyes to Jesus, tears slowly streaking her cheeks as sadness overwhelmed her. Her shoulders heaved slightly as a silent sob escaped through trembling lips. Jesus watched silently as her pain deepened.

"One morning not long after, Sarah told me with a sneer that Abraham wanted to talk with Ishmael and me, nodding toward the edge of the clan settlement. Abraham was already there, sitting alone. 'What about?' I asked, but she wouldn't say and turned her back to me. So Ishmael and I set out to join Abraham. He stood, his eyes teary. He gave Ishmael a long embrace, then hugged me and then another long embrace with Ishmael. It was very confusing. He asked us to sit as he reached for a light tote bag and a flask, and then he sat."

She closed her eyes and began to sob as the memories flooded over her. Jesus sat alongside, placing his arm around her shoulders. Her head found his shoulder, the tears falling onto his tunic. Tenderness filled his eyes as the sobbing continued. Gradually, the sobs softened, replaced by quiet sighs and tears.

Her head still on his shoulder, she continued, "Abraham said that for reasons he couldn't explain, Ishmael and I must leave and no longer be part of the family. I cried and begged, but it didn't make any difference. Ishmael sat in disbelief, shocked that his father would reject him. Abraham stood, gave me the bread and water, and pointed to the wilderness as our home from then on. He also said he was confident that his God would take care of us. Then he turned and walked away. He just turned his back to us and left us there. We could not go back, he said, because we were no longer welcome." With a deep sigh the tears stopped, her head resting on his shoulder.

"'Father, come back!' Ishmael yelled, but Abraham just kept walking. 'Father, why have you rejected us?' he called louder. Still no reaction. 'My father, why have you forsaken me?' he wailed, but Abraham never looked back. Ishmael looked at me, tears streaming down his face, and cried, 'Mama, what did I do?' And I had no answers for him."

They sat quietly. Jesus withdrew his arm as she lifted her head, dabbing her eyes with the fold of her wrap.

"I'm sorry, Jesus," she said meekly. "It took me a long time to get past the pain of utter rejection. When the one who has been your mainstay, your provider, rejects you, well, the pain is unbearable. I never hated Abraham for the rejection. Yet I lived with that pain, the hopelessness, for the rest of my life. It never left me."

"But God did take care of you, Hagar," Jesus noted softly, "and Ishmael. You returned to Egypt, Ishmael found a wife, and had many children and became the father of a great nation, just as God promised.[30] So things turned out all right, didn't they?"

Hagar looked at him, then rose and stared across the landscape. "If progeny is the measure of blessing, Jesus," she replied coldly, "then God favored Ishmael and me as promised." She turned and stared at him, all tenderness gone. "So was the promise kept? Yes…but the promise did not salve the wound of utter rejection. Even Ishmael, I think, carried a bitterness within him for many years. He loved his father so much, but he never could understand why a father would reject his son—especially his firstborn.

"When I became Abram's wife and the mother of his son, all the people—the entire clan—were overcome with joy. I had not only become accepted, but Ishmael and I grew to be favored by those closest to us—by Abram and Sarai. The people loved and respected us and adored Ishmael.

"It is one thing to be rejected by the people around you who were the first to accept you and, eventually, who favored you above all others. That rejection stung. That was the wound of my rejection. Ishmael's rejection was far more devastating. He had been rejected by his father. Of all people, his father. And the scar of that rejection never left."

They sat silently. Gradually, Hagar's eyes softened. "The only thing Michael could tell me, Jesus, is that you seem to be searching for something during these days in the wilderness. I'm not sure I have helped you. The part of my story which seems to interest you most is the darkest part of my memory. Is there something else you seek?"

---

[30] Genesis 21:17–21

Jesus smiled. "You have helped me more than you know. Thank you. I am sorry if reliving those memories brought back the pain."

"Well, it is beyond my understanding how my story could be of help." She smiled. "Can you enlighten me?"

"You sound like Michael," Jesus chuckled and paused. "I am yet uncertain how these days in the wilderness will end. But to live within time and experience fully the struggles of humanity, I must undergo the same trials and the same joys. Otherwise, how could I really know the height and depth of the life of man?

"If the joy of overwhelming acceptance and the pain of utter rejection is in my future, I must be prepared not to waver in order to fulfill the purpose for entering time as a human. Your story helps me to understand," he concluded.

"And what is that purpose?" Hagar asked.

Jesus smiled. "That's what Michael wants to know."

*****

After Hagar left, Jesus and the pup remained in solitude in the shadow of the crag for several hours. Though he seemed in high spirits when he returned at sunset, it was clear to Michael he had been moved by the conversation. To Michael's pleasant surprise, Jesus opened up.

"You know, Michael," he began after settling at the pool's edge, dabbling his feet, "Hagar and Ishmael's story recorded in the sacred scrolls is passed over too quickly." He paused as though mesmerized by the gentle swirls. "How could the father of a firstborn son, a son he professes to love deeply, later abandon that son? How could a loving father turn his back and walk away, utterly rejecting his son, and never speak to him again? Ishmael was on the cusp of manhood, the time when a son most needs a father's guidance and insight. And Abraham walked away." He turned to Michael, who was resting against the tree with the pup lying beside him. "Why would a father do that?" he asked.

Michael studied his face. It was clear that Jesus was genuinely troubled. "You have been blessed with a loving father in Joseph, haven't you?" Michael asked. "Can you imagine anything that would cause Joseph to behave like that?"

Jesus leaned over and picked up a flat stone, juggled it a couple times, then skipped it across the pond. He sat silently, studying the widening ripples. "That is my problem," he said, tossing a second stone. "No, I cannot. I cannot imagine a loving father walking away from his son." He stared at the ripples until they had faded completely, then turned his eyes to the golden remnant of day's end spanning the distant horizon. "The grief and fear which gripped Ishmael as he called out his last words to the father he loved have shaken me."

"What were those words?" Michael asked pensively.

Jesus stared into the distance and softly replied, "'My father, why have you forsaken me?'"

DAY 28

Rest

On the seventh day, he rested.

DAY 29

The Satan
Temptation of Michael

"I wondered if you would show," the satan began. "Actually, I'm a little surprised. You were never the kind to go off on your own. Always the loyal servant." He smirked. "Don't get me wrong. There's nothing wrong with loyalty. I'm surrounded by it!"

Michael's eyes were fixed upward on the far limbs of the old oak. "He said there would be no harm in it, so that's why I'm here. Jesus was curious what you might have to say to me." He turned to Storm who was reclined against the trunk. "But I'm not." Slowly, his gaze returned to the gnarled limbs. "We've never been 'close,' if you know what I mean. So why are we here?"

The heat of the day had passed as the sun approached the horizon; the gentle breeze was refreshing. Similarities in build were amplified by their attire—both clad in simple loincloths, loose linen tunics, and sandals. Michael feigned disinterest in the small cooking fire nearby, the twin freshly baked loaves of bread, and the wine—though the aroma was hard to ignore.

The satan smiled. "Let's enjoy the bread while it's fresh," he said, motioning to the smooth stones arranged for seating. "There is no reason we can't be civil to each other and enjoy some conversation without being at each other's throats. Who knows, we might find we have more in common than we realize." The satan broke the closest loaf and tore off a piece. "Mmmm…fresh bread. Nothing satisfies better." He smiled.

Michael watched cautiously, his defenses alert. Yet the hospitality extended by Storm seemed genuine, and the aroma was enticing. "Okay," he said, sitting on the second stone. "But don't be offended if I seem more than a little suspicious. If there is one thing I've observed about the earthly realm, your motives are never as pure or innocent as they seem. Never. In the end, someone is always hurt. You seem to take pleasure in that." He lifted the second loaf and lingered over its warmth and aroma, then broke off a piece and dipped it in the wine. "Almost heavenly," he sighed. Another piece followed the first and then another. After a deeper sip of wine, the goblet found its way back to the makeshift table. Michael shifted to the soft sand and leaned against the stone. "I must compliment you. The combination of the bread and wine is excellent."

"I am glad you like it." The satan smiled. "So did Jesus. He found it quite satisfying in fact." The goblet was poised at his lips, his eyes intently on Michael. "But of course, you know all about that."

Michael turned his head to avoid Storm's eyes, looking pensively at the lowering sun. His mind was racing, trying to imagine Storm's intent in this time together. The discomfort didn't seem to be shared by the satan. Silence surrounded them—for Michael, an uncomfortable silence.

"You *do* know all about that, don't you?" the satan asked with a slight tease, enjoying Michael's discomfort. "I *am* curious. How did Jesus describe our first encounter here? Was there a sense of longing in his eyes or in his tone of voice?" He was studying Michael's face as he raised the goblet for another sip.

Michael's eyes turned slowly back to the lowering sun, avoiding Storm. Once more, silence.

"Come on, Michael. What did he say? You can tell me. Remember, I was there, so nothing would surprise me," he pressed. "What was his mood when he returned?" A slight grin had crossed his face. The satan was enjoying Michael's discomfort.

Michael took a slow, deep breath. "He didn't say anything," he sighed, searching the horizon. "So you're wasting your time. Why don't you tell me what happened?" His eyes sought Storm's. "He was sound asleep when I found him the next morning, lying right over there," he pointed several paces distant. "For being under the tree all night, he seemed quite refreshed. He was quiet on the walk back, his mind seemingly on other things." The satan raised an eyebrow as Michael continued, "When I pressed, Jesus just smiled and quickened his pace. That's all I know."

The satan grinned, delighting in this news. "He never told you," he cackled. "Well, well. That is very interesting. He never told you." Now it was *his* eyes which turned toward the late-day sun nearing the horizon. "Most interesting," he repeated slowly. He turned back to Michael. "Would you like to know about that evening? Are you curious what happened? As his loyal servant, surely you would want to know." He paused. "In fact, if he has kept you in the dark, then you don't know his deepest needs." His eyes were fixed on Michael, whose focus remained on the horizon. "I'm surprised, Michael. How can you serve him completely unless you know his deepest needs? Does that seem fair to you, especially with all the things you are asked to do? Does it seem fair that he would keep you from knowing his deepest needs? After all, you are his most trusted servant, are you not?" The satan paused to let his words sink in, then continued in a tone of incredulity, "Does that seem right, if you are the one he trusts above all others?"

For a moment, Michael sat still. "I've never given it much thought," he replied quietly. "I have always trusted him to confide the things I need to know. Anything else is none of my business. If he wanted me to know, he would tell me."

"Well, what about the visit a few days ago," Storm continued, "when we were once again in this place. Did he tell you about that? Surely Jesus must have said something about that conversation."

Michael glanced overhead, feigning disinterest.

"You *are* the one he trusts completely, aren't you?" the satan probed. "He *always* turns to you in matters of highest importance, doesn't he? Aren't you his most trusted one? And if you are, why wouldn't he bring you into his confidence now? Has he told you about his plan?"

Michael fell silent, the questions hanging in the air. He reached for the bread, dipped a piece in the wine, savored it, and followed with a slow, full swallow of the enchanting wine. A second morsel followed, as did a second swallow of wine. The question gnawed at him: "But you are the one he trusts completely, aren't you?" As the third swallow lingered, a sense of unease surrounded him. *Why hadn't Jesus confided in me?* he wondered. *Why hadn't he?* It was an obvious question which had never occurred to him.

The satan was watching closely as Michael wavered. "Well, it's not important," the satan continued nonchalantly, riveted on Michael's countenance. "I was just curious." He raised the goblet with a nod toward Michael's. He turned toward the setting sun and quietly observed, "Soon the day will end." Michael returned the nod and took another sip. "I had hoped to learn whether Jesus enjoyed our first time together, and if he had any thoughts on the second," said the satan wistfully as silence returned.

"No matter," he reflected, turning his gaze back to Michael. "You know, Michael, I have a confession to make." Michael turned aside, again feigning disinterest. The satan smiled, eyes riveted on Michael. "I have long admired you, with just a touch of envy. I have admired your devotion to I Am—and now even more, realizing that I Am doesn't confide fully in you. That devotion is even more admirable." The satan paused, letting the words have their effect.

Michael hadn't moved, his eyes focused on the sun as it approached the horizon, the sky transformed to a golden hue. Storm's words were discomforting.

The satan's gaze intensified. "There's a place for you here, Michael," he said, "a place of highest honor—a place where your special relationship with I Am would be of immeasurable worth, a place that even I Am would honor and admire." The satan paused, watching intently—but Michael remained unmoved. "We both know the depth of I Am's love for this earthly creation and, above all, for humanity. I Am's heart is embedded within humanity. But we both know that when I am shackled creation with time, a barrier was formed which humanity cannot cross. Mankind cannot attain to the heavenly realm, and that reality causes pain in the heart of man.

I see the pain. I hear their cries." He was watching Michael closely. "Through the generations, my steadfast presence has helped them live with that pain. Yet I grieve for them as they strive to live into the joy of the heavenly realm but with no hope. Their pain is my pain."

Michael turned toward Storm, his wariness overcome with sadness—sadness for the plight of humanity. Storm's confessions were opening his eyes to an earthly reality he had never considered. Of course, he had watched the pain humanity had long endured. But the premise that the pain was rooted in the I Am-established barrier to heavenly joy had never occurred to him. Even more, the premise that Storm experiences pain when humanity suffers was contrary to all of his instincts of the satan reveling in their misery. Perhaps his distrust of Storm had been wrong all along.

The satan sensed Michael's uncertainty. "We can change it all, Michael. Together, we can change it." His tone was earnest, sincere. "My legions and I are consumed with the cries of humanity as time ravages their lives. When I Am entrusted the earthly realm to my care, I didn't grasp the immensity. I realize now—as I watch you and the I Am man, Jesus—I have failed in my relationship with I Am. I have focused all my energy and resource on humanity within the earthly realm, oblivious to the importance of nurturing my relationship with I Am." The satan paused, watching for a hint of acceptance and understanding from Michael.

Indeed, Michael's stare had softened. The confession of Storm revealed a character he had never seen or imagined. But the satan was making sense. There *was* much pain and suffering in the world, pain and suffering which could be eliminated if humanity were to experience the heavenly joy. Surely I Am would agree with that—and yes, it is understandable that the fullness of Storm's resources would be consumed by the need of a humanity shackled by time.

The satan sensed the time was right. "You enjoy a rare privilege, Michael—the freedom to engage in this realm and also within the heavenly realm and the limitless presence with I Am. I could enjoy that presence too—if I were not so fully consumed with care for the earthly realm.

"Humanity needs you, Michael. I need you. Together, we can change humanity and remove its suffering. You would be the trusted emissary with I Am, and we would share the full power over the earthly realm. Your hand and voice within the presence of I Am would change everything here.

"Join me...and together we will change the world."

Michael was stunned—never could he have imagined such a proposal! He was speechless as the proposal sank in. Together with Storm—end human suffering? Be the sole emissary between the two realms as I Am's trusted servant? He reached for the goblet, sipped, and sat silently, deep in thought.

The satan was pleased...and took the bread, followed by a sip of wine. Michael's silence signaled the strength of the satan's persuasive powers. Perhaps this was going to be easier than he had imagined. What a victory were Michael to come over.

"I don't know," Michael began slowly. "It is true that I Am has entrusted me with the rare privilege of servanthood, trusted and unquestioning, but it would come as no surprise even to you that I Am is suspicious of your motives. So it would be understandable that I might be a little suspicious."

"You have every reason to be," the satan replied, "because you have only seen one side of me. The side you haven't seen, the side I have revealed to you here, is my true self. I Am knows this side of me. Why do you think Jesus encouraged you to meet with me?"

That's a good question, Michael thought. There was a depth and understanding in Storm's answers.

"This is all a part of I Am's plan, Michael. Jesus knows that, but he couldn't explain it to you, which is why you have been so confused. I Am and I had agreed that I would be the one to make the proposal. I Am, as the man Jesus, wanted you to experience my sincerity. Jesus trusts you—and he trusts your judgment. He will be waiting for your return with open arms and with joy."

Michael was perplexed. *Could it be that I have been misjudging Storm all along?* he wondered. Storm's eyes were fixed on him in eager anticipation—an unsettling anticipation.

Suddenly, instinct and certainty gripped Michael; his countenance changed. The Master of Deceit had nearly convinced him! He stood, his eyes locked on Storm's. "You have spoken one truth, Storm: I Am—Jesus—trusts me." He paused. In a sneer of disgust, he exclaimed, "But all else are lies—and *I don't trust you!*" With an abrupt pivot to return to Jesus, Michael strode away briskly as the sun slipped below the crimson horizon.

"Your only chance, Michael," Storm shrieked after him. "You will regret this forever!" The rage Michael had seen so many times now consumed the satan as the ground shook, lightning danced, and thunder rolled.

The satan had failed.

DAY 30

Hosea
The Priesthood and Religion

"He was here only a few days ago?" he asked, clearly disappointed. "Why wasn't I invited earlier, Michael?" he cried. "The old-timers told lots of stories about Elijah, even though most of them were only toddlers when he was around, but the tales they told," Hosea exclaimed, "I would have given anything to grill him on some of his experiences."

"Well, it's probably just as well you weren't here," Michael chuckled. "Jesus had him pretty well buttonholed. I doubt you'd have had much time with him, and then you would have been even more frustrated."

"Do you know what they talked about? You know, I lived about two or three generations after Elijah, and none of the prophets who came after him, me included, could hold a candle to his reputation or his powers, but it sure would have been fun to compare notes. By the time I came around, the people—even the priests—had strayed further from the teachings and commands of the prophets. It seemed like I spent most of my time warning them about the consequence of their turning away from the Lord's commands," he reflected, "not a lot of time teaching. From the looks of things not much has changed." He stopped and fell silent, squinting his eyes and peering across the desert emptiness toward the lone figure far ahead.

His low, gravelly voice well-suited a dark leathery face. Beneath thinning gray brows, creases accented gray-green eyes and framed his weathered lips. He shuffled more than walked, with a slight stoop. The knotty walking stick gripped tightly in his age-spotted right hand had been polished from years of use. A faded loose-fitting tunic secured by a belt at the waist hung just past his knees, well short of the worn sandals. The darkened skin of his bald crown had borne the brunt of years of sun and wind. Below the crown, a thin mantle of gray hair brushed his shoulders and seemingly wrapped around his jaw into a thin scraggly beard.

Hosea had been thrilled at Michael's beckoning to return to the folds of time at the bidding of the man, Jesus. "But why as an old man?" Michael had asked. "All others have returned to time physically vibrant, but here you are, wracked with old age. I guess I should have made it more clear. It is curious though—why come back as an old man?"

The grizzled man smiled as he pointed with the cane to the distant Jesus, holding Michael's arm with his free hand to steady himself. "You told me Jesus was a young man, didn't you?" He grinned. "I've had many experiences dealing with young men. They don't listen very well, but as I grew old, they seemed to think they needed to pay attention because of my 'wisdom.'" His eyes were fixed on Jesus who was slowly making his way toward them, the young jackal dancing about him. "Ah, he has a dog," Hosea exclaimed. "You didn't tell me there'd be a dog." He lowered the cane and shook it as though in warning. "Good thing I brought my trusty crutch," he declared. "It's kept many a dog away from these old legs."

"Oh, I don't think you need to worry about the pup," Michael chuckled. "She's harmless, and he delights in her. They seem to have been attracted to each other. I imagine by the time Jesus gets here, she'll be spent and will wander off to rest." Jesus paused to wave at them, then turned and tossed a sun-bleached bone for the pup to fetch. They laughed as the cycle repeated over and over.

"I see," chuckled Hosea. "You're right. That pup doesn't look dangerous. Maybe a little mischievous, but not a threat."

"So you want to impress Jesus with your wisdom, is that it?" Michael teased.

"Can't hurt," Hosea replied. "Anyway, in an odd way, it's good to be back in the old body and feel the aches of advancing years, but I'm curious. What does he want with me?"

"I don't know what Jesus has in mind during the time with you. We'll find out soon enough," Michael said as Jesus neared. The pup had indeed wandered off to find shade and rest.

As Jesus approached, the old man dropped his cane and fell to his knees, his head bowed and hands clasped at his chest. Emotion had overtaken him. "My Lord, it is a humble privilege to return to time at your invitation and be with you," he said, his raspy voice quavering.

Jesus reached down and took his clasped hands, raising him to his feet. "My friend," he said, embracing him warmly. "The privilege is mine. Thank you for returning and enduring time once again." Jesus stepped back, looking closely at Hosea. He turned to Michael. "Did you explain he could return at any age? And I thought we were to meet at the pool in the shade of the tree."

"Well, I guess the first part was an oversight." Michael smiled, nodding toward Hosea. "No matter. He's enjoying himself, cane and all. He wanted to return like this," he said, waving his hand from Hosea's foot to his head. "And he has a pretty good reason."

Jesus turned back to Hosea. "And what would that be, my learned friend?" he asked, intrigued. "And to make things less formal, please call me *Jesus*, the name my father gave me. We're here as peers, Hosea." Jesus smiled. "A couple men chatting about what has been and what may come. Okay?"

In earlier times, Hosea would have looked Jesus squarely in the eye, but the passing years had shortened his frame, even more with the stoop, so that he had to tilt his head upward. "Ah, yes," Hosea said softly, "Michael had said to call you *Jesus*." He closed his eyes, stood silently for a moment, and sighed deeply. "In my day, the name *Jesus* would have meant *Yahweh saves*." Slowly, he opened his eyes. "Do you think that is what your father had in mind when he gave you that name?" He was studying Jesus's face.

"That's a good question, Hosea." Jesus smiled and turned toward Michael. "Let's ask Michael. He was there."

Michael nodded thoughtfully. "Well, I think so, Hosea—at least, indirectly. I was instructed to visit Joseph in a dream and tell him to name his son Jesus 'because he will save his people from their sins.'[31] So that's what Joseph did—and here stands the man, Jesus."

Hosea leaned forward and peered pensively into Jesus's eyes, steadying himself with the cane. With his free hand, he grasped Jesus's right hand. "You do not have an easy path ahead, young man. Do you know that?" His eyes were earnest, moist.

Jesus held the withered hand gently and looked tenderly into the wizened eyes. "That's why you are here, my aged friend. By listening to your struggles, I hope to learn a little about what the future may hold." Holding the old man's hand, he turned to Michael. "It's a far distance to the pool and the shade of the tree. Do you have a plan where we might sit and talk?"

Hosea interrupted, tugging Jesus's hand. "No, Michael, let me." He smiled. "I told Michael I wanted to walk in the desert for a time, to be reminded of its heat and feel the dryness in my throat. We can talk on the way—at my pace. There should be plenty of time. Will you indulge the request of an old man?" The twinkle in his eyes belied his age.

*****

Both Jesus and Michael were enthralled by the mental clarity of the elderly man. As Jesus probed deeper and deeper, Hosea described in fascinating detail the misdeeds and errors of the people and his growing frustration with their obstinacy. "They just would not listen," he sighed. "Time after time, they would not listen—and it only caused them more pain. I was obedient to the call of the Lord, declaring the instructions I had been given, but it was like shouting into the wind. The people were determined to go their own way and ignore the teachings handed down to them through the prophets."

---

[31] Matthew 1:21

"What do you mean, Hosea?" Jesus asked. "What do you mean, that they were 'determined to go their own way'? Was it all the people? And what was *the way* they wanted to go?"

There was a fire in Hosea's eyes. Reliving the past had stirred something inside as though he were back in the midst of the upheavals. Now for a change, in Jesus and Michael was an audience interested in what he had to say.

"Well, you may remember," Hosea replied, "that in those days, the nation had split years before into two nations because of loyalties to differing ideologies—and loyalties to the leaders who sprang from them. People had become more entrenched in their own ways of thinking, unwilling to listen to those who didn't agree with them. By my time, the differences were beyond reconciling. The lines were too firmly drawn.

"Gradually, the wisdom of the ages…of the prophets…was rendered old fashioned. More and more, the people embraced the latest 'truths' which suited them—and followed leaders who rode the false 'truths' to power. The new 'truths' satisfied their individual wants but ignored the less fortunate on the margins. The soul of the nation was foundering. No one was calling them back to the time-tested teachings—teachings of God at the center and concern for neighbor.

"No one, that is, but me. I was the lone voice, the lone messenger obedient to God's instructions. Yet the people went their own way. As I said, it was like shouting into the wind. Nothing changed." Hosea fell silent, overcome with sadness in recalling the fruitlessness of his efforts. "No one listened, and nothing changed," he repeated softly.

As the emotion in Hosea's story grew, their pace had slowed and now stopped. Jesus and Michael had been listening quietly, watching the pain crease Hosea's face in the telling. Whether from the telling or the distance, it was taking its toll on the old man. Fortunately, the oasis with its water and shade was not far.

"But what about the priests?" Michael asked. "They were schooled in the wisdom of the prophets. Surely they too were calling the people to reconcile with each other, and with God."

Hosea turned toward the distant tree and resumed the slow pace. "You would think so, but sadly, no." he sighed. "A few were faithful, but their voices were drowned out by the many. Most of the priests had become caught up in the culture of the times and had abandoned the ancient teachings. They relished the attention of the leaders and enjoyed being seen with them. To gain their favor, they parroted the mantras of the day. As time went by, it became more important to preserve their standing than to call for a return to the age-old truths. In order to preserve the institution of their religion, they abandoned the teachings on which it had been built. The religion—the faith—no longer mirrored its teachings.

"The people were perishing as knowledge of the old truths faded. The priesthood had lost their way, and the people suffered. That was the message God instructed me to tell the priests.[32] When the religious institutions cave to the culture, the people suffer and the soul of the nation cries. Eventually, the people came back to God, but only after enduring much hardship," he said with an air of sadness, slowly shaking his head.

They had reached the pool. Michael cupped his hands into the cool water and lifted them to the old man's lips. He took a sip, and then another. "The people suffered so much pain," Hosea continued. "If only the priests had been true to the prophets and the people had listened to the Voice of the Ages. From what you have shared, Michael, the times are not much different today."

Leaning on his cane and spent from the exertion of the day—but with a fire in his eyes—the old man turned to Jesus and asked, "Will you be that voice, Jesus? Will you be the one to challenge their spiritual laziness and call them back to the age-old truths?"

---

[32] Hosea 4:6

DAY 31

Michael and the Satan Refusal

Gabriel wasn't pleased, but he had no choice. He knew that Michael's orders had the blessing of I Am. So he had delivered the message to the satan to meet Michael once again under the petrified oak. Now Storm had been waiting; at last, Michael had arrived.

"What is it now, Michael?" the satan asked curtly. "I am not in the habit of engaging with those who reject me."

"It was Jesus's idea," Michael replied. "He didn't think it would take long—"

Before Michael could continue, the satan interrupted with a look of surprised anticipation. "Aah! You've changed your mind! Jesus explained, and you've changed your mind," he cried. "You didn't need to send Gabriel for that! You should have come directly. Why keep me waiting?" He was elated. "This is great, great news!"

Smug delight had overtaken the satan. A thin smile creased Michael's face. "Oh, Storm…how satisfying this is…" He paused.

"A feat never to be equaled," the satan gloated. "My powers of persuasion, unparalleled. Surely envy rests in the heart of I Am." He leaped to his feet, dancing in perverse jubilation. "Do you grasp the immensity of what I have accomplished?" he shouted, the ground trembling underfoot.

Michael had not moved, quietly relishing what was to come. The satan was oblivious to his presence. Michael waited.

"Isn't it a great plan, Michael? You must be very curious about how we will set all this in motion, right?" the satan cried. He was quivering with excitement, his eyes returning to Michael. "Aren't you?" he asked, now realizing that Michael hadn't moved.

"Not really, no," Michael replied. "I'm not in the least curious. You see, Storm, once again, I am just the messenger. Jesus asked me to deliver his answer to your 'magnanimous' proposal of immortality." Michael slowed, poised to fully enjoy the moment ahead.

"No," Michael declared calmly. "There is no way Jesus will ever align with you. His answer is no."

Michael spun on his heels and left, the predictable fury and rage thundering across the desert emptiness. His satisfaction was complete.

DAYS 32, 33, 34

Jesus
Solitude and Fasting

My father, why have you forsaken me?

The words of Ishmael continued to unsettle Jesus though he didn't know why. Every once in a while they would echo softly in the still of the outcropping. Something about them haunted him. Even with the fullness of I AM, the heaviness within would not leave.

The words of the sage priest further burdened him. The old truth-teller seemed to describe the very same emptiness coming from the lips of the synagogue leaders he had left behind in Nazareth. How could hope be restored to them and, through them, to the people?

And of course, the satan. The dilemma of the satan.

DAY 35

Rest

On the seventh day, he rested.

DAY 36

Michael and the Satan
The End Is Near

"You sicken me!" the satan hissed between clenched teeth. "Jesus...I AM...whatever you're calling him these days...it all sickens me. But above all, you. I despise you even more than I despise I AM, your holier-than-thou deference to Jesus. You sicken me." Storm seethed with an icy hatred. The piercing glare of the steel-cold eyes was unsettling.

"Has it been fun, Michael, these little games you've been playing?" he sneered. "Is there any meaningful purpose to what the all-powerful Man God has been doing these past weeks? Have you enjoyed being his lackey?" The contempt was deep-seated. "You sicken me." He seethed as he turned his back, glaring across the emptiness and beyond the far horizon. Iciness surrounded him.

Michael was unmoved. It wasn't hatred which gripped him. It was weariness. He was exhausted. Time had that effect on him, which Storm mistook as weakness. Michael's words were measured. "The end is near," he said firmly. "Though before Jesus leaves this place and returns to fully man, you will meet again. Tomorrow. Here." He couldn't help the satisfaction of delivering the message. It wasn't as much as being I AM's most trusted messenger as it was the pleasure of the effect any message had on Storm.

The reaction caught him short. The deep-seated anger and icy hatred immediately gave way to tenderness, and a smile of genuine warmth filled Storm's eyes. Kindness seemed to radiate. Michael stiffened. Across the eons of time, he had witnessed and experienced the disarming nature of Storm—the master of false love, of counterfeit compassion—and humanity was always the loser. Always.

Storm had changed in an instant, but why? "So the end is near," Storm repeated thoughtfully. "What does this mean 'before Jesus leaves this place and returns to fully man'? Did he say that? Were those his words?" His eyes were smiling, a warmth in his tone.

"Those were Jesus's words, Storm," Michael acknowledged guardedly. "'The end is near.'"

"And 'before he leaves this place'…?" The words came slowly from his lips, his eyes softening as he stared absently past Michael. "'Before he leaves this place'…" he repeated softly. "You know I Am as well as any heavenly or earthly being, Michael. Yet even you seem bewildered these last weeks. Do you know?" Storm's tone was genuine. "Has he told you why these past weeks? Has he told you why he came? More importantly, has he told you why he wants to see me?"

Silence surrounded them as Michael studied him. "No, he hasn't," Michael replied. "But you already know that since everything in the earthly realm is within your grasp." He sneered. "You have heard Jesus encourage me to be patient in the midst of my confusion. And you have heard him say that in time I will understand, though I still don't."

"Well, if the end of his little earthly jaunt is near, I'll be glad," said Storm, a hint of hiss returning. "And if tomorrow brings that time closer, this world will be the better for it."

DAY 37

The Satan
Charlatan of Deception

Control is the key, he thought. Ever since time began, ever since he had fallen awry of I AM, control had been the key. Yes, I AM had removed him from the heavenly realm, but having power over the earthly realm without himself being constrained by time had softened the banishment. And while it was not possible for him to bask in the heavenly realm, there were endless encounters with the heavenly beings. Of course, it was unfair that I AM had given freedom across both realms to the heavenly beings and not to him. Even so, in the earthly realm, control was the key. And having power in the lives of all earthly creatures—especially humanity—well, control is the key. I AM had not taken that from him.

The setting under the ancient oak in the midst of the forsaken desert seemed somehow appropriate. It was where this had all begun. If the end was coming, how appropriate—to end where it began.

He was leaning against a boulder with his eyes on the far horizon, the same horizon over which Jesus had come the first time. No games today. The satan had grown weary of the games. Jesus, or I AM, or whoever he wanted to be called this time—no games. Besides, Jesus hadn't been playing by the rules. Maybe that is what kept drawing the satan back to each encounter—the mystery—each testing the other, yet Jesus always parting unshaken, while the satan always left conflicted. No doubt about it, Jesus was unlike any other man the satan had encountered in all of history. Until now, everyone had played by the satan's rules—and his rules always prevailed. Always.

Until now. Oh, his control over the earthly realm hadn't waned. Only here—in this place and with this man—had his control wavered. Yet his confidence was unshaken. He knew in the end his control would prevail. That was the deal. That's always been the deal. And if there was one certainty in this cosmic dance since the beginning of time, it hinged on the parting assurance of I Am: "You are free to exert your will in the earthly realm."

The lone figure was approaching, his sandaled feet at a measured pace. The sand-colored tunic blended with the desert background, contrasting the bronze tone of the exposed skin. His eyes were fixed on the satan—not in defiance or fear, instead, purposeful.

The satan waited, black silk robe wafting gently about him in the midday breeze. Something was different: for the first time, he was feeling ill at ease. In the previous encounters, he had always felt in control—or at the least, equal. This time, an air of uncertainty had come upon him, and he was confused.

"Michael says your time here is coming to an end," he noted smugly, ignoring Jesus's outstretched arms as he approached. "There is no need for that," nodding to the outstretched arms, "We're not brothers and certainly not long-lost friends." He was unmoved, still leaning against the rock, emotionless eyes fixed on Jesus.

Jesus smiled. "You've carried bitterness for a long time, my friend," he said, slowly lowering his arms.

"Please!" the satan reacted sarcastically. "Friend? I choose my friends, and you are not one of them, nor will you ever be! Let's be clear on that—and let's get on with whatever brings you here. If the end is near, I'll accept your goodbye, and you can leave."

Jesus slowly walked past the rock and approached the ancient oak, looking upward into the gnarled limbs. He placed his hands on the stone trunk, eyes following it upward. "Why have you left this here?" he asked, staring into the outstretched branches. "Why through the ages have you left this remnant of long ago?" He turned toward the satan and settled to the ground. "Does it remind you of something?"

"What is that to you?" the satan sneered. "I have the power to save or destroy in my realm, and I have no one to answer for it. Not even you." He paused. A wicked smile crossed his face. "Or have you forgotten your pledge?"

There was no reaction from Jesus which, in that instant, seemed peculiar to Storm. It was as though Jesus had no recollection of I Am's promise when the satan had been relegated to the earthly realm. Could it be that I Am had not, after all, come into time in this man, Jesus? Maybe that explained Michael's confusion; maybe Michael wasn't as close to I Am as he had always presumed. More important, maybe there was no mystical connection between this Jesus and the mighty I Am! He waited as Jesus silently stared upward, eyes fixed on the twisted limbs against the cloudless sky.

Impatiently the satan leaned forward. "That's it, isn't it?" he exclaimed. "You are not I Am after all!" His eyes danced with certainty, delighting in his newfound truth. "That's why Michael doesn't understand! You've deceived him all along, and all these 'assignments' have been to test him—to test his loyalty to this grand deception." A satisfied laugh erupted from deep within. "Oh my, how grand a deception after all! Even beyond my imagining. I can't wait to see Michael's reaction when he figures out how little loyalty is worth to the mighty I Am." He reveled in the thought.

With no warning, storm clouds billowed over the horizon and began their march toward the ancient oak. Lightning flashed as thunder rolled across the desert. "I'll be leaving then," the satan snarled. "There is no reason to play your game, you charlatan of deception." He turned to walk toward the black roiling cloud now almost upon them. "You will not last in my domain," he bellowed above the thunder and wind as the guttural laugh returned.

"You will not last!" It echoed again and again and again as the thunder became one with the guttural laugh.

*****

173

"What do you mean he left?" Michael exclaimed in bewilderment.

Jesus grinned. "That's exactly what I meant. He left! Before I could answer, his storm chariot was upon us, and he left. I guess he can be a little short-tempered." He laughed.

DAYS 38, 39

Waiting

The air had turned cold, the wind biting. Something had riled Storm, of that Michael was certain. In the day since the abrupt parting, Jesus had turned silent, his face set on the distant horizon as though it weren't there. 'Let him storm,' Jesus had said. The fury and bitter cold intensified and stretched across two days.

DAY 40

Morning
Michael, the Satan, and I Am—Perdition[33]

Finally, Michael thought. *Finally*.

"Go to the abode of the satan and alert him to my coming," Jesus had instructed.

"When will that be?" Michael had asked.

"Just go," Jesus instructed with an air of impatience.

It was a place I Am had declared off limits to the heavenly beings—a place where the satan and his devoted legions would be undisturbed, a place devoid of life, devoid of good. From horizon to horizon, in every direction, dreariness—brambles, rocks, a frigid wind. At its core was an ominous cavern from which hordes of demons frenetically raced to and from the furthest ends of the earth. Ghastly, hideous demons—neither human nor heavenly—were too numerous to count, in blind obedience to their master.

As Michael approached, the demons bellowed their warning, louder and louder. Abruptly, Storm appeared before him clad in a dingy loincloth with a defiant glare. Anger swept from the steel-gray eyes, muscles tense in anticipation.

"You are never to be here," he seethed. "That was the promise, Michael. None of you, ever, in this place. Take your ragged whatev-

---

[33] Perdition—a noun. In ancient traditions: the netherworld; the abode of the dead; a place of final spiritual ruin.

176

er-you-are back to the *holy* realm," he mocked, "wherever that is. And take that imposter, Jesus, with you." The anger peaked. "Leave now, or you will *never* leave!"

"Do you think I *want* to be here?" Michael sneered as their eyes met, the hatred between them intensifying. "I have come to deliver a message, and then I will leave."

"Well then, deliver it," Storm seethed. "Deliver it and go!"

"He is coming here. Very soon," Michael declared and turned to leave. "Any moment."

"Who is—"

Suddenly, an intense calm enveloped them, rendering Storm speechless. The demons had vanished. A mistlike blanket draped the landscape and stretched in every direction beyond the horizon. Slowly—silently—the mist drew toward them, gathering into an indistinct spirit-like shape, a featureless pulsating wispy, translucent presence that danced in the desert calm seemingly within reach, yet beyond their grasp. They stood transfixed by the movement of the Spirit, awash in the peace of its pulsating glow. The presence was mysterious, rhythmically swaying as in a breeze, yet seemingly invisible—simultaneously seen and unseen. As the last tendrils of mist drew in, the surrounding desert began to fade. Soon only the satan, Michael, and the pulsating Presence remained amidst the nothingness. Time stopped.

Michael bowed deeply and fell to his knees. The satan trembled and froze—unable to move—remaining upright in the grip of the pulsating glow.

"Do not be afraid," a voice emanated from the Presence, a voice of comfort, of purpose, of power. Softly, the voice continued, "Thank you, Michael, my beloved. You may go."

Slowly, Michael rose, bowed once more, turned, and vanished—leaving only the satan in the presence of I Am.

DAY 40

Noon
I AM and the Satan—Restoration

"So this is how it all ends," the satan declared defiantly, mustering courage in the presence of I AM. In the certainty of pending doom, anger had left. With his eyes set firmly on the essence before him, the satan would not submit—not even in what assuredly were these final moments.

The pulsating rhythm of the Presence slowed, the satan awash in its radiance.

"Little has changed, has it, my friend," the voice of I AM came, softly. "Little has changed." Silence filled the space between them. Then from the depth of the Presence, a sorrowful sigh rooted in agony. "I had hoped for contrition. Instead, bitterness has deepened—and with it, pain. Pain has deepened. Because of your bitterness, humanity—indeed, the fullness of creation—writhes in pain."

Silence lingered as the radiance softened.

"*My friend?*" retorted the satan. "None of this was of my doing, Most High." Sensing the end may not be as imminent as he had feared, the satan continued, "Just remember, it was *your* breath that brought it all into being. First the heavenly realm—and then as we watched in awe, the wonder of the earthly realm. You breathed everything into being. For whatever brokenness there may be within that 'holy plan,' you have only yourself to blame. *You* rejected *me*, remember? So yes, I confess that bitterness lies deep within me. It is bitterness that sustains me, that gives me purpose. And if my bitterness causes pain in your humanity, well, so be it. That pain is where I find my joy. Even more so now, knowing that their suffering brings you pain."

Again, silence. The glow of the Presence softened further.

"Michael was right, you know," the satan continued. "When you turned me away, my only desire—my sole purpose—became to wound you at your very essence. Indeed, to wound the heart of God. Knowing that you suffer whenever one of your beloved humans suffers…even if only one…well, I am now overflowing with gratitude. You have gladdened my heart, confirming that you suffer."

Silence returned. Only silence enveloped the satan and the soft glow of the Presence.

Slowly, the rhythmic sway and its radiance began to return. "I have never regretted," the Presence began wistfully, "imparting the freedom of will to the heavenly and earthly beings. Never—not even to you. When a being experiences the exhilaration of that freedom, my heart sings. How could I withhold such a gift and deprive myself of that joy?"

The radiance and the rhythm intensified. "When you chose to lure the earthly ones to follow you, I grieved deeply—for you and for them. It grieved me to impose the shackles of time on the earthly beings—and to relegate you to the earthly realm along with those heavenly beings who chose to follow you. Your choice, and the choices of all who follow you, stained the beauty of creation as I intended."

"Well, Mighty One," the satan taunted, "if it grieves you so, unstain it! If all power rests in you, then you have the power to set it right, don't you?" He paused. "So set it right, and restore humanity to that mystical oneness you grieve for. Set it right, and free me from the perpetual hell of these selfish beings you created."

As the tone of the satan moved from taunt to confrontation, the nature of the Presence slowly began to change, gradually assuming a human shape. The glow intensified as the rhythmic swaying ceased. Now in the midst of the nothingness, only the satan and I Am, in the form of a transfigured Jesus, remained.

"My friend," Jesus began warmly, "perhaps you will be more at ease with me in human form. There is no need for confrontation."

Visibly shaken by the presence of the transfigured Jesus before him, the satan recoiled and stumbled backward, uncertain of what lay ahead. Yes, this was the Jesus he had encountered, but this time, somehow different. A man, yes…but something more. A warmth seemed to flow from him, almost tenderness, a presence from which the satan had long ago departed. Now as it enveloped him, it stirred memories long buried, memories of vulnerability, memories which ended in pain.

"Charlatan of deception," Jesus chuckled. "That was a good one. I had to laugh. You, *Delilah*? Talk about deception! *Charlatan of deception*, indeed!" Jesus's eyes twinkled as he laughed.

The satan, without lowering his guard, joined in the laughter. "Yes, that was a good one. And for a brief moment, I thought I had you with Delilah. You nearly fell for her, didn't you? We came so close." He grinned.

"Oh yes, it was an evening I won't forget, to be sure, an important evening to learn your ways firsthand." Jesus smiled, reflecting on the experience. He paused. "The mind and heart of man alone is no match for you and your legions. Your power over humanity is beyond their understanding. They have been tantalized through your craftiness by false understanding. Sadly, they place certainty in the power of their own thinking, little realizing that you are at the root of those thoughts. Left alone, none can prevail against you. And that, my friend, is the stain on humanity. Your bitterness and the pain it inflicts is the stain. You are the stain." Jesus had turned somber.

Not the satan. He was no longer wary. No, it was becoming clear he had misjudged this encounter with I Am. For if I Am's intent was to destroy the satan, there would have been no need or purpose for dialogue. No reason for a forty-day wilderness journey. A solitary breath of obliteration would have sufficed. No, there was more.

Intrigue gripped the satan. What was in the mind of the transfigured One standing silently before him in the midst of cosmic nothingness? All of creation had been swept away. No heavenly hosts, no Michael or Gabriel, no wild beasts at Jesus's beck and call—only the satan and I Am in the form of the transfigured Jesus.

And then it came to him. "Ah, now I see your struggle," the satan began with a sly smirk. "It is regret, regret and remorse over your created plaything. You are consumed by regret. That's it, isn't it, Jesus? You, the great I Am, suffering from a twinge of regret over the stained humanity you created. Regret is one of my favorites because it always leads to despair. *If only I had done it differently*, is it?" he observed wryly. "So *that* is where your pain lies." His finger pointed with conviction.

Jesus turned toward the satan, tenderness in his eyes. "No, my friend, you are wrong. You misjudge me yet again. Regret is not at the root of my pain. There is nothing I regret over what I have created and in what continues to unfold. Quite the contrary, that is the source of my deepest joy: the fullness of all creation. Even this," Jesus continued. He raised his arms, and suddenly, all around had been restored to the place they had left. The two were standing on the brink of the satan's cavernous abode surrounded by an icy silence. All was still. The demonic horde, eerily silent, was riveted on the unfolding drama of the duo at its center.

"Surely, Jesus...I Am—you regret the gift of free will and its consequences. After all, it was in your *infinite wisdom*"—the satan sneered—"that the purity of the *great plan* was foiled. Why not take it back? Is that why you have come into the earthly realm...*my* realm...to retrieve your tainted gift? If that is so, just take it and be done. Take back the tainted gift, eliminate me, and leave. How long must humanity linger?" The satan seethed with hate. "Wave your magic arm, retrieve free will, obliterate me and this hell on earth, and leave!" Suddenly, bedlam was all around as the demon horde roared its guttural approval, awed by the temerity of the satan. The emboldened horde swarmed about them, hurling taunt after taunt at the stoic Jesus.

Slowly, silently, Jesus turned and faced the horde. Under his hypnotic stare the multitude cowered as the warmth of his transfigured presence enveloped them, serenity and peace restored.

"I can see why Michael calls you *Storm*," he said, studying them. "The legions worship your destructive powers. They yearn for more, so you satisfy their selfish desire to fuel their loyalty. It is an endless cycle of hate, bitterness, and pain." He paused. "Perhaps they will embrace another way—the way of shalom, the way of harmony, of peace." The radiance surrounding his presence intensified.

"You underestimate me, Jesus, and them. There is nothing other than me—nothing and no one—they will follow or pledge their loyalty to, only me," the satan boasted. "They have witnessed my absolute power over this realm. They are instruments of that power. No one, not even you or your omnipotence, can sway their loyalty. You may be the great I Am in your domain, but not here. Not in the eyes of these minions. Their loyalty to me is absolute." He snarled and unleashed a haunting, hideous shrill of contempt which reverberated across the landscape and through time.

The legions stirred but remained silent, transfixed by the contrast of the dark passion of their satan and the calm, resolute confidence of the transfigured One. It was as though all of time had been building to this moment, and they were witnesses to it.

Quiet returned. The outer calm of the satan belied his inner turmoil. He too sensed the magnitude of the moment unfolding, but it was the *not knowing* that had him unsettled. In this realm, in *his* realm, he was in charge. Yet something was shifting, and the uncertainty of what was to come was his discomfort.

Jesus peered deeply into the eyes of the satan—past the bluster, past the hurt, past all the transgressions of time. In that moment, the satan felt vulnerable.

"My beloved," Jesus began, arms outstretched, the Presence a blend of human and the ethereal I Am enveloped in an indescribable affection. "I have come into the earthly realm not to destroy but to restore. Not to set aside free will but to set it aright, to restore all humanity, indeed the whole of creation, to all I had intended. And above all, to restore you, to bring you and your followers home—into the arms of all the hosts in the heavenly realm.

"They long for you. I long for you. They love you. I love you. I have never stopped loving you. It is time for you to come home—and with all the hosts, restore creation and humanity to the joy I intended.

"Come home, my beloved. Come into the arms of my love."

DAY 40

Afternoon
Turndown

Storm was dumbfounded—shocked!

He stumbled, lost his balance, fell backward—away from Jesus's outstretched arms—and crumpled to the ground, dazed. His mind was reeling. What had just happened? None of this made sense. He sat up and coughed to clear his head.

How long had he lain there? He didn't know. Michael had returned, and he and Jesus were squatted nearby. Jesus was speaking in low tones; Michael was staring at Storm, smiling. The hordes had retreated, quietly watching from a distance. All was still.

Michael rose, walked to Storm's side, and sat down. "You okay?" he asked with a smile. Storm glanced toward Jesus who was lying on the ground on his side, watching them.

One thing had not changed: his disdain for Michael. That hatred was deep-seated. Storm's icy glare erased the smile on Michael's face, and his guard returned. If the love of I Am had warmed the heart of the satan, there was none extended to Michael. But this was not a time for caution.

"I Am yearns for you, brother. Come home. Accept the gift of I Am's love. No conditions. Simply accept and come home. Do not spurn his love this time, my friend. I Am's deep desire is for your return to the heavenly realm. Let the vibrancy of I Am's joy abound— and restore all creation to the fullness of its intended beauty."

For a moment, the glare softened. Storm's attention turned to Jesus who had risen and was slowly walking toward him. Their eyes met—the boundless love of I Am radiant. Perhaps all *could* be restored. He rose to receive the outstretched arms and the embrace which would sweep aside all past wrongs.

But the hurt...the rejection...was too deeply engrained. It defined him. Shaken, he turned to sift through the confusion and clear his mind. It *was* in that rejection that his power rested. Yes, he had long ago rejected I Am, but when I Am cast him away from favored status—from the heavenly realm—the raw, festering wound defined him for all time, time filled with torment, spilling into humanity. In the power of human suffering, he had found pleasure—a pleasure to transcend time.

The hardened glare returned, his face twisted by hate. With an abrupt pivot, he spun to confront the One who was the cause of his eternal pain. To accept his embrace would mean forgiving I Am for the humiliation he had endured. He could never return. Never.

An icy wind began to blow, and the demon horde stirred. Black terrifying clouds rushed to consume them with unmatched fury. His body contorted in rage, Storm's clenched fist rose defiantly in the space between them. Jesus paused, his tender gaze unfazed. Driven by rage, Storm extended his arm and pointed at Jesus, an icy finger inches from his face.

"SCREW YOU!" he bellowed, the words reverberating across his realm. The demon horde erupted as lightning thundered, and the ground shook.

DAY 40

Midnight
Promise Kept

The gnarled oak loomed against the black sky, jagged limbs painted by the silver moon. In the shadows, three were gathered: the cloaked one, Jesus, and the satan. The tone was subdued.

That had not been so earlier. At I Am's direction, Michael had approached Storm to arrange this final meeting as midnight approached—the enmity between them now more deeply rooted. It amused the satan that Michael yet again had no insight as to why they were gathered.

"You ignorant, dutiful stupe," Storm had sneered. "If I Am was going to destroy me, it would have already happened. So why the invitation? I Am can offer nothing I want." Michael had remained silent.

The satan's rejection of the invitation to full restoration had saddened I Am, though it had not come as a surprise. No, the sadness which filled I Am was not because of the refusal. Rather, it was because earthly suffering would continue. So now it was time to put in motion another path to restore humanity.

Storm stood defiantly, ignoring Michael nearby, his icy stare fixed on Jesus standing before him. Jesus's eyes, tender yet firm, focused on Storm.

"How much longer, Jesus? How many more of these little trysts am I going to have to endure? That little invitation to 'come home' was cute, but let's move on," Storm sneered impatiently. "Let's put an end to this." As he was speaking, the radiance of the transfigured Jesus returned. The satan fell silent.

Softly, I AM began. "My heart continues to grieve over you, my beloved—that has not changed. I had hoped that creation could be restored, beginning with you." I AM paused. "But you make your choices, so my grieving—and earthly suffering—continues."

Slowly, a self-satisfied smirk creased Storm's face. "Well, I AM, you hold all power, or so you have led us to believe. Change it. Destroy me and put things back to your grand plan. But do it now. If you can."

Silence surrounded them. In the quiet space, warmth flowed from I AM. The silence hung in the air.

The satan was unmoved. "Ahhh, I see," Storm began slowly, his eyes widening. "In this moment, it has become clear to me." I AM was silent, tenderness flowing—but to no effect on Storm. "You *won't* destroy me. You *can't* destroy me—because deep within all that omnipotence, you are flawed." He taunted slowly, the sneer returning. "The great I AM—flawed!"

Michael was horror-stricken. Yet I AM remained silent, unmoved.

The silence emboldened the satan. He turned to Michael. "You don't get it, do you, you worthless dolt," he sneered. "You are too blind to see it!" His gaze returned to I AM. "You can't destroy me because of *love*! Your stupid love gets in the way." He cackled, the hideous laughter reverberating across the empty wasteland. "A most fateful flaw—the Almighty, powerless in love!" He was convulsed by his own sinister scorn.

Slowly, the echoes faded. Silence returned.

The radiant countenance of I AM in the form of Jesus had not changed. His tender, purposeful gaze remained fixed on Storm. "Yes," I AM began, "love is my core. I *am* love. Everything I have created has been created in love—even you, my son. Even you. Whether you accept it or not, you are an inheritor of my love—as you shall always be—you, Michael, Gabriel, and all the heavenly hosts, as with all those in the earthly realm. My love surrounds all. It lives in and through all, even you, though you have chosen to reject it."

"Well, just remember," the satan retorted, "*you* cast me out. *You* put me here and forbid my return. And *you* gave me power over this realm." He waved his outstretched arm across the wasteland. "That was your promise." He glared. "Or are you going to break your promise? Is that why we are here? Will you no longer keep your promise?" He seethed.

Turning to Michael, I AM's eyes softened. "I wanted you here, Michael, so you would understand." Michael had been silent, observing all. The love flowing from I AM, surrounding Storm and him, was overpowering—beyond anything he had experienced.

I AM's gaze returned to the satan. "No, my beloved," I AM began slowly. "The promises I made remain, but I wanted you to hear this from me, which is why Michael arranged this last time for us together: It is my will and my ultimate joy to restore humankind to the fullness I intended from the beginning. However, since you have chosen to remain in the earthly realm, suffering will continue to plague them because that is your delight.

"Even so, I will no longer leave them alone, subject solely to your will. I will gather a handful and show them the way to right living and teach them my truths—truths which they will teach others—truths which will pass from generation to generation through a community unbound by time, a community anchored in my love. I will come to them in Spirit in every generation so that all will receive power to turn from you and, in turning from you, to receive hope. In that hope they will find inner peace in lives of purpose and joy, even amidst the suffering you will inflict."

The satan was silent, absorbing every word.

I AM continued, "At the end, I will remove the one power from you which lies at the root of humankind's deepest fear: the power of death. No longer will you be able to control their lives through that ultimate fear—the fear of dying. They will receive life—eternal life, even here in this earthly realm—and my joy will be complete."

When I AM stopped speaking, the radiance surrounding the transfigured Jesus faded, leaving Jesus, the man; Storm, the satan; and Michael.

"So how are you going to accomplish all that?" Storm asked sarcastically. "Humanity never learns."

"Wait and see," Jesus said, staring into the eyes of the satan. "Wait and see."

Then turning to Michael, he said, "It's time, Michael. We have things to do. It's time to change the world."

And they left.

EPILOGUE

The satan's sole purpose is to wound the heart of God.

Jesus lay in silence, reclining on a bed of leaves in the shade of the fruit tree at the pool's edge. The words Michael had spoken weeks ago reverberated through his mind. *Wound the heart of God.* The satan had no idea the depth of pain in I Am 's heart from this last rejection. Jesus was overcome by an emptiness and deep sadness that his plan to restore the satan—indeed, all humanity—had failed. The satan's choice to once again reject I Am meant that suffering would continue across all mankind. Jesus wept.

Michael watched quietly. In the thirty years he had been entrusted with Jesus's care, he had never witnessed such grief. At the moment, it was difficult for him to separate Jesus the man from Jesus the I Am. He could recall only one instance when I Am had grieved so deeply: the moment the satan chose to depart from the divine will. I Am knew then what lay ahead for beloved humanity. Now Jesus— the man and the I Am—grieved once again for humanity and for the satan. The pain I Am was feeling was Michael's pain.

After a time, Jesus sat up. The soft rustle through the overhead leaves and gently rippling water helped to ease the pain. He breathed deeply, then turned toward Michael. "All is not lost, Michael." His voice was filled with compassion as he surveyed the surroundings. "You have served well," he complimented. "Thank you."

"May I say, Lord," Michael replied quietly, "that the breadth and depth of your love is beyond my understanding. It has no bounds, even in the midst of deepest pain. It is very difficult to watch your grieving, realizing that your grief for humanity and for the satan is the same. It is beyond my understanding."

Jesus smiled. "Love is the easy part, Michael. Grieving only deepens the love." He sat quietly.

"Well, I guess now I know the plan." Michael smiled. "All along, you planned to restore Storm, didn't you? That was the plan, wasn't it?"

"Yes, now you know," Jesus chuckled. "Yet you are probably wondering why the visits with Moses and all the others. Have you figured that out?" he asked.

"Some of it, I think," Michael reflected. "I think that while your desire was that Storm would accept and return to the heavenly realm, you weren't so sure given his history. So that part makes sense, but I'm not sure of the rest."

"That's fair, Michael. How could you be sure?" Jesus paused. "Your supposition is correct. I was hopeful the satan would accept my invitation—so very hopeful. But as you said, he exercises free will in ways which grieve me. *Wound my heart*, as you put it. So while the overriding plan was for the satan's restoration, at the same time, I wanted to prepare for the alternate plan if the first one failed. The visits were part of that."

He sat quietly, reflecting, and continued, "With the satan remaining in the earthly realm, the suffering of humanity continues. As the satan said, he knows me too well. He knows the depth of my love—and that the sure way to the vulnerability of my heart is through humanity. Even so, it remains my deep desire to restore all of them to the place intended when I created them, male and female: that *all* of humanity may be one with me.[34]

"When the satan stained the gift of free will and was relegated to the earthly realm, the stain took root in humankind. That gift brings me great joy when humanity exercises it for good—and the satan knows that. He also knows that choosing harm or ill will toward others grieves me, and that delights him. And so the age-old human conflict through all of time: the choice of good or evil and its consequence.

[34] John 17:22–23

"You know, Michael, that the weapons of the satan in this conflict are manifold. They are most often rooted in behaviors which harm or hurt. In dialogue with those you hosted, I wanted to gain a deeper understanding of a few of these devastating behaviors: doubt undermining purpose, pride inflating self, the craving for adulation, power used to harm, subjugation of the other."

Though hanging on every word, Michael was confused. "Why, Jesus? For what purpose?" he asked. "We have watched these struggles from the beginning of time. What could you possibly learn that we haven't observed across every generation of humanity?"

Jesus smiled. "Ah, Michael, an excellent question. It is precisely why these interactions were essential for what lies ahead." He paused and dipped his hand in the cool water, then splashed his face. "You will soon return to the heavenly realm. Before you do, how about one last memory of this special place?" he invited, splashing his face again, then playfully tossing handfuls at Michael.

Michael ducked and laughed at Jesus's impishness. Some of the water hit its mark. "An interesting choice, Jesus, tossing the water. Was that choice for good or evil?" Jesus joined in the laughter.

They sat quietly for a few minutes, both reflecting on the time together during these forty days. Then Michael continued, "So back to my question, Jesus. Why the conversations? How could you learn anything that you didn't already know? We have observed these behaviors since the beginning of time. So for what purpose?"

Jesus's gaze had turned to the far side of the pond where the young jackal was splashing in and out, in frenzied pursuit of a frog. Michael joined in the laughter. In surrender, the pup collapsed on the shore, its tongue hanging and sides heaving to catch its breath. Time for rest.

His eyes on the pup, Jesus replied, "I have learned many things, Michael, living within time as a man. It is one thing to observe the influence of the satan from the heavenly realm, but it is far different to *live* under that influence—to experience the consequence of a decision and *feel* its effect. I wanted to engage with some who had lived the experience and felt the pain of their choices—and perhaps to experience it and feel it myself. Why, you might ask?" He paused, turning to Michael. "Because of what lies ahead. Storm's refusal doesn't mean humanity has been abandoned to his ways. You heard a little of that in the final exchange with the satan. Do you recall?"

"I do, Jesus," Michael replied, "but it was brief, and I must confess I was absorbed by the shock of Storm's refusal. You were quick to move past that, but I wasn't. So I might have missed a few things. I think you intimated what the future holds—both for Storm and for humanity. Am I right?"

"Indeed you are." Jesus smiled. "Now let me be more specific because I will need your help far more in what lies ahead, along with all the heavenly realm.

"To set the plan in motion, I will leave here and return to the shore of the Jordan and continue from there as the man, Jesus, but things will be different. No more carpenter's bench, no more rabbinical 'preparation'. From this moment, my days will be grounded in I AM's *promise* of restoration—a *promise* of a future and of hope, of teaching how to live within this *promise* while enduring the pain and suffering of the world.

"In the days to come, I will gather a handful of twelve followers[35]—apostles, they will be called—and teach them, over and over, the essential truths of what it means to live within the *promise*: to love God and to love their neighbor. They will learn and teach that to love their neighbor is as simple as to treat others as you wish to be treated.[36] They will become my witnesses across the land[37]—and receive power to heal, power to loosen the grip of the satan's legions, and power to proclaim the essential truths in every circumstance with conviction in the face of rejection.

"Great crowds will follow them, Michael—and me. Sadly, the people's desires will be focused on worldly things—like healing their sick, feeding their hungry and poor, and shedding their oppression by Rome. As their demands and desires grow, it will take all my willpower to stay true to this plan—true to my purpose—to turn away

---

[35] Matthew 10:2–4
[36] Luke 6:31
[37] Acts 1:8

from doubt, resist their adulation, challenge misguided religious authorities, and deny their expectation of a powerful king. I will be placing all of my trust in you and the heavenly realm to keep me steadfast."

Michael was transfixed. "You said something about death and the fear of dying, Jesus. What did you mean?"

Jesus turned somber, his eyes fixed on Michael. "This is how I will change the world, Michael—and all of humanity," he said slowly. "I will remove the satan's control over death and dying. No longer need humanity fear dying because they will know that in dying, new life comes, that death is not the end but rather the gateway to new life with me."

"How, Jesus?" Michael asked, bewildered. "How will you do that?"

"I will die," Jesus replied.

Shock overtook Michael. His face twisted; his eyes bulged. "What does that mean?" he gasped. "I don't understand that. Do you mean that you, the man Jesus, will *die*?" he exclaimed.

"I will die," Jesus repeated. "This body. My essence. I will die."

Michael fell to his knees, confused and overwhelmed.

"Fear not, Michael," Jesus declared with conviction in his eyes. "I will rise from the dead—from the grip of the satan and his hell—and return to the living.[38] From the moment of my resurrection, the satan and all humanity will know that the power of death has been removed from his grasp, that the old death is no more because all will rise to new life after dying to this one.

"And here is the best news. I Am knows that no human can withstand the cunning, the trickery, the deceitful ways of the satan—no human. It is beyond human ability to resist his every whim. And so this new gift—the new gift of the risen life—is for everyone, no matter the missteps when within the satan's grasp." Jesus placed his hands on the crown of Michael's head. "I Am's love extends to all. No one is denied the new life that is assured by my dying and my rising—no one."

---

[38] John 20:1–18

Michael rose. Overcome with emotion, he wrapped Jesus in his arms and sobbed. In deep compassion, Jesus returned the embrace.

"Our time here is finished, Michael," Jesus said. "The twelve are awaiting my call. After my dying and my rising, they will go tell and teach all people this good news.[39] And I will send my Essence—the Spirit of truth—to them, and the world will begin to change.[40] From that moment and for all time, those who believe and follow me will receive the very same Spirit, along with the hope and the *promise*, which will change the world."

Turning, they were no more. The barren desert yielded no clue of pool or tree, only a lone young jackal meandering across the empty wasteland.

---

[39] Matthew 28:18–20
[40] John 16:13–15

WORDS FOR REFLECTION

In the beginning God created the heavens and the earth. (Genesis 1:1 NASB)[41]

In the beginning was the Word, and the Word was with God, and the Word was God. He was in the beginning with God. All things came to be through him, and without him nothing came to be. What came to be through him was life, and this life was the light of the human race; the light shines in the darkness, and the darkness has not overcome it. A man named John was sent from God. He came for testimony, to testify to the light, so that all might believe through him. He was not the light, but came to testify to the light. The true light, which enlightens everyone, was coming into the world. (John 1:1–9 NAB)[42]

When God in the beginning created man, he made him subject to his own free choice. If you choose, you can keep the commandments; it is loyalty to do his will. There are set before you fire and water; to whichever you choose, stretch

41 New American Standard Bible, The Lockman Foundation, PO Box 2279, La Habra CA 90632, http://lockman.org.
42 The New American Bible, World Catholic Press, a Division of Catholic Book Publishing Corp.

forth your hand. Before men are life and death, whichever he chooses shall be given him. (Sirach 15:14–17 NAB)

It is enough to recall that in the final analysis the demon has no power over us but what our freedom is willing to grant him. (Father Serge-Thomas Bonino, *Magnificat*, September 1, 2020)[43]

Lord, sustain me as you have promised, that I may live! Do not let my hope be crushed. (Psalm 119:116 NLT)[44]

"For I know the plans I have for you," declares the LORD, "plans to prosper you and not to harm you, plans to give you hope and a future." (Jeremiah 29:11 NIV)[45]

Do not let your hearts be troubled. Believe in God, believe also in me. (The words of Jesus, John 14:1 NRSV)[46]

Jesus Christ is the center of history. God entered the history of humanity. Through the Incarnation, God gave human life the dimension that he intended man to have from his first beginning. (John Paul II, *Magnificat*, September 25, 2020)

---

[43] Magnificat, Inc., 86 Main Street, Yonkers NY 10701. www.magnificat.com.
[44] New Living Translation, Tyndale House Publishers, Inc., PO Box 80, Wheaton IL 60189.
[45] New International Version. International Bible Society, Zondervan Publishing, 5300 Patterson Avenue, S.E., Grand Rapids MI 49530.
[46] New Revised Standard Version, Division of Christian Education of the National Council of Churches of Christ in the USA.

Now to him who by the power at work within us is able to accomplish abundantly far more than all we can ask or imagine, to him be glory in the church and in Christ Jesus to all generations, forever and ever. Amen. (Ephesians 3:20 NRSV)

For through faith you are all children of God in Christ Jesus. There is neither Jew nor Greek, there is neither slave nor free person, there is not male and female; for you are all one in Christ Jesus. (Galatians 3:29 NAB)

Our calling is not primarily to be holy men and women, but to be proclaimers of the Gospel of God. (Oswald Chambers, *My Utmost for His Highest*, January 31)[47]

---

[47] Oswald Chambers, *My Utmost for His Highest*, Discovery House Publishers, Box 3566, Grand Rapids MI 49501. Published by Barbour Publishing, Inc., PO Box 719, Uhrichsville OH 44683 www.barbourbooks.com.

APPENDIX

For convenience, the enumerated footnotes with corresponding biblical texts follow.

(All texts are from the New Revised Standard Version (NRSV) Bible, copyright 1989, the Division of Christian Education of the National Council of the Churches of Christ in the United States of America.)

1. *Philippians 2:5–8a.* "Let the same mind be in you that was in Christ Jesus, who, though he was in the form of God, did not regard equality with God as something to be exploited, but emptied himself, taking the form of a slave, being born in human likeness. And being found in human form, he humbled himself and became obedient to the point of death—even death on a cross."

2. *Matthew 3:13–15.* "Then Jesus came from Galilee to John at the Jordan, to be baptized by him. John would have prevented him, saying, 'I need to be baptized by you, and do you come to me?' But Jesus answered him, 'Let it be so now; for it is proper for us in this way to fulfill all righteousness.' Then he consented."

3. *Genesis 2:8–9.* "And the LORD God planted a garden in Eden, in the east; and there he put the man whom he had formed. Out of the ground the LORD God made to grow every tree that is pleasant to the sight and good for food, the tree of life also in the midst of the garden, and the tree of the knowledge of good and evil."

4. *Matthew 1:21.* "She will bear a son, and you are to name him Jesus, for he will save his people from their sins."

5. *Exodus 3:11–14.* "But Moses said to God, 'Who am I that I should go to Pharaoh, and bring the Israelites out of Egypt?' He said, 'I will be with you; and this shall be the sign for you that it is I who sent you: when you have brought the people out of Egypt, you shall worship God on this mountain.' But Moses said to God, 'If I come to the Israelites and say to them, "The God of your ancestors has sent me to you," and they ask me, "What is his name?" what shall I say to them?' God said to Moses, 'I AM WHO I AM.' He said further, 'Thus you shall say to the Israelites, "I AM has sent me to you."'"

6. *Exodus 2:10.* "When the child grew up, she brought him to Pharaoh's daughter, and she took him as her son. She named him Moses, 'because,' she said, 'I drew him out of the water.'"

7. *Exodus 2:1–3.* "Now a man from the house of Levi went and married a Levite woman. The woman conceived and bore a son; and when she saw that he was a fine baby, she hid him three months. When she could hide him no longer she got a papyrus basket for him, and plastered it with bitumen and pitch; she put the child in it and placed it among the reeds on the bank of the river."

8. *Exodus 3:1–2.* "Moses was keeping the flock of his father-in-law Jethro, the priest of Midian; he led his flock beyond the wilderness, and came to Horeb, the mountain of God. There the angel of the LORD appeared to him in a flame of fire out of a bush; he looked, and the bush was blazing, yet it was not consumed."

9. *Luke 2:41–51.* "Now every year his parents went to Jerusalem for the festival of the Passover. And when he was twelve years old, they went up as usual for the festival. When the festival was ended and they started to return, the boy Jesus stayed behind in Jerusalem, but his parents did not know it. Assuming that he was in the group of travelers, they went a day's journey. Then they started to look for him among their relatives and friends. When they did not find

him, they returned to Jerusalem to search for him. After three days they found him in the temple, sitting among the teachers, listening to them and asking them questions. And all who heard him were amazed at his understanding and his answers. When his parents saw him they were astonished; and his mother said to him, 'Child, why have you treated us like this? Look, your father and I have been searching for you in great anxiety.' He said to them, 'Why were you searching for me? Did you not know that I must be in my Father's house?' But they did not understand what he said to them. Then he went down with them and came to Nazareth, and was obedient to them. His mother treasured all these things in her heart."

10. *Exodus 16:13.* "In the evening quails came up and covered the camp; and in the morning there was a layer of dew around the camp."

11. *Genesis 3:23–24.* "Therefore the LORD God sent him forth from the garden of Eden, to till the ground from which he was taken. He drove out the man; and at the east of the garden of Eden he placed the cherubim, and a sword flaming and turning to guard the way to the tree of life."

12. *Exodus 20:8–11.* "Remember the sabbath day, and keep it holy. Six days you shall labor and do all your work. But the seventh day is a sabbath to the LORD your God; you shall not do any work—you, your son or your daughter, your male or female slave, your livestock, or the alien resident in your towns. For in six days the LORD made heaven and earth, the sea, and all that is in them, but rested the seventh day; therefore the LORD blessed the sabbath day and consecrated it."

13. *Matthew 2:13–16.* "Now after they had left, an angel of the Lord appeared to Joseph in a dream and said, 'Get up, take the child and his mother, and flee to Egypt, and remain there until I tell you; for Herod is about to search for the child, to destroy him.' Then Joseph got up, took the child and his mother by night, and went to Egypt, and remained

there until the death of Herod. This was to fulfill what had been spoken by the Lord through the prophet, 'Out of Egypt I have called my son.' When Herod saw that he had been tricked by the wise men, he was infuriated, and he sent and killed all the children in and around Bethlehem who were two years old or under, according to the time that he had learned from the wise men.'"

14. *Judges 16:4–21.* "After this he fell in love with a woman in the valley of Sorek, whose name was Delilah. The lords of the Philistines came to her and said to her, 'Coax him, and find out what makes his strength so great, and how we may overpower him, so that we may bind him in order to subdue him; and we will each give you eleven hundred pieces of silver.' So Delilah said to Samson, 'Please tell me what makes your strength so great, and how you could be bound, so that one could subdue you.' Samson said to her, 'If they bind me with seven fresh bowstrings that are not dried out, then I shall become weak, and be like anyone else.' Then the lords of the Philistines brought her seven fresh bowstrings that had not dried out, and she bound him with them. While men were lying in wait in an inner chamber, she said to him, 'The Philistines are upon you, Samson!' But he snapped the bowstrings, as a strand of fiber snaps when it touches the fire. So the secret of his strength was not known. Then Delilah said to Samson, 'You have mocked me and told me lies; please tell me how you could be bound.' He said to her, 'If they bind me with new ropes that have not been used, then I shall become weak, and be like anyone else.' So Delilah took new ropes and bound him with them, and said to him, 'The Philistines are upon you, Samson!' (The men lying in wait were in an inner chamber.) But he snapped the ropes off his arms like a thread. Then Delilah said to Samson, 'Until now you have mocked me and told me lies; tell me how you could be bound.' He said to her, 'If you weave the seven locks of my head with the web and make it tight with

the pin, then I shall become weak, and be like anyone else.' So while he slept, Delilah took the seven locks of his head and wove them into the web, and made them tight with the pin. Then she said to him, 'The Philistines are upon you, Samson!' But he awoke from his sleep, and pulled away the pin, the loom, and the web. Then she said to him, 'How can you say, "I love you," when your heart is not with me? You have mocked me three times now and have not told me what makes your strength so great.' Finally, after she had nagged him with her words day after day, and pestered him, he was tired to death. So he told her his whole secret, and said to her, 'A razor has never come upon my head; for I have been a nazirite to God from my mother's womb. If my head were shaved, then my strength would leave me; I would become weak, and be like anyone else.' When Delilah realized that he had told her his whole secret, she sent and called the lords of the Philistines, saying, 'This time come up, for he has told his whole secret to me.' Then the lords of the Philistines came up to her, and brought the money in their hands. She let him fall asleep on her lap; and she called a man, and had him shave off the seven locks of his head. He began to weaken, and his strength left him. Then she said, 'The Philistines are upon you, Samson!' When he awoke from his sleep, he thought, 'I will go out as at other times, and shake myself free.' But he did not know that the LORD had left him. So the Philistines seized him and gouged out his eyes. They brought him down to Gaza and bound him with bronze shackles; and he ground at the mill in the prison."

15. *Numbers 20:12.* "But the LORD said to Moses and Aaron, 'Because you did not trust in me, to show my holiness before the eyes of the Israelites, therefore you shall not bring this assembly into the land that I have given them.'

16. *Sirach 15:14.* "It was he who created humankind in the beginning, and he left them in the power of their own free choice."

17. *1 Samuel 16:1–13*. "The LORD said to Samuel, 'How long will you grieve over Saul? I have rejected him from being king over Israel. Fill your horn with oil and set out; I will send you to Jesse the Bethlehemite, for I have provided for myself a king among his sons.' Samuel said, 'How can I go? If Saul hears of it, he will kill me.' And the LORD said, 'Take a heifer with you, and say, "I have come to sacrifice to the LORD." Invite Jesse to the sacrifice, and I will show you what you shall do; and you shall anoint for me the one whom I name to you.' Samuel did what the LORD commanded, and came to Bethlehem. The elders of the city came to meet him trembling, and said, 'Do you come peaceably?' He said, 'Peaceably; I have come to sacrifice to the LORD; sanctify yourselves and come with me to the sacrifice.' And he sanctified Jesse and his sons and invited them to the sacrifice. When they came, he looked on Eliab and thought, 'Surely the LORD's anointed is now before the LORD.' But the LORD said to Samuel, 'Do not look on his appearance or on the height of his stature, because I have rejected him; for the LORD does not see as mortals see; they look on the outward appearance, but the LORD looks on the heart.' Then Jesse called Abinadab, and made him pass before Samuel. He said, 'Neither has the LORD chosen this one.' Then Jesse made Shammah pass by. And he said, 'Neither has the LORD chosen this one.' Jesse made seven of his sons pass before Samuel, and Samuel said to Jesse, 'The LORD has not chosen any of these.' Samuel said to Jesse, 'Are all your sons here?' And he said, 'There remains yet the youngest, but he is keeping the sheep.' And Samuel said to Jesse, 'Send and bring him; for we will not sit down until he comes here.' He sent and brought him in. Now he was ruddy, and had beautiful eyes, and was handsome. The LORD said, 'Rise and anoint him; for this is the one.' Then Samuel took the horn of oil, and anointed him in the presence of his brothers; and the spirit of the LORD came

mightily upon David from that day forward. Samuel then set out and went to Ramah."

18. *1 Samuel 17:4–51*. "And there came out from the camp of the Philistines a champion named Goliath, of Gath, whose height was six cubits and a span. He had a helmet of bronze on his head, and he was armed with a coat of mail; the weight of the coat was five thousand shekels of bronze. He had greaves of bronze on his legs and a javelin of bronze slung between his shoulders. The shaft of his spear was like a weaver's beam, and his spear's head weighed six hundred shekels of iron; and his shield-bearer went before him. He stood and shouted to the ranks of Israel, 'Why have you come out to draw up for battle? Am I not a Philistine, and are you not servants of Saul? Choose a man for yourselves, and let him come down to me. If he is able to fight with me and kill me, then we will be your servants; but if I prevail against him and kill him, then you shall be our servants and serve us.' And the Philistine said, 'Today I defy the ranks of Israel! Give me a man, that we may fight together.' When Saul and all Israel heard these words of the Philistine, they were dismayed and greatly afraid. Now David was the son of an Ephrathite of Bethlehem in Judah, named Jesse, who had eight sons. In the days of Saul the man was already old and advanced in years. The three eldest sons of Jesse had followed Saul to the battle; the names of his three sons who went to the battle were Eliab the firstborn, and next to him Abinadab, and the third Shammah. David was the youngest; the three eldest followed Saul, but David went back and forth from Saul to feed his father's sheep at Bethlehem. For forty days the Philistine came forward and took his stand, morning and evening. Jesse said to his son David, 'Take for your brothers an ephah of this parched grain and these ten loaves, and carry them quickly to the camp to your brothers; also take these ten cheeses to the commander of their thousand. See how your brothers fare, and bring some token from them.' Now Saul, and they, and all

the men of Israel, were in the valley of Elah, fighting with the Philistines. David rose early in the morning, left the sheep with a keeper, took the provisions, and went as Jesse had commanded him. He came to the encampment as the army was going forth to the battle line, shouting the war cry. Israel and the Philistines drew up for battle, army against army. David left the things in charge of the keeper of the baggage, ran to the ranks, and went and greeted his brothers. As he talked with them, the champion, the Philistine of Gath, Goliath by name, came up out of the ranks of the Philistines, and spoke the same words as before. And David heard him. All the Israelites, when they saw the man, fled from him and were very much afraid. The Israelites said, 'Have you seen this man who has come up? Surely he has come up to defy Israel. The king will greatly enrich the man who kills him, and will give him his daughter and make his family free in Israel.' David said to the men who stood by him, 'What shall be done for the man who kills this Philistine, and takes away the reproach from Israel? For who is this uncircumcised Philistine that he should defy the armies of the living God?' The people answered him in the same way, 'So shall it be done for the man who kills him.' His eldest brother Eliab heard him talking to the men; and Eliab's anger was kindled against David. He said, 'Why have you come down? With whom have you left those few sheep in the wilderness? I know your presumption and the evil of your heart; for you have come down just to see the battle.' David said, 'What have I done now? It was only a question.' He turned away from him toward another and spoke in the same way; and the people answered him again as before. When the words that David spoke were heard, they repeated them before Saul; and he sent for him. David said to Saul, 'Let no one's heart fail because of him; your servant will go and fight with this Philistine.' Saul said to David, 'You are not able to go against this Philistine to fight with him; for you are just a boy, and he has been a warrior from his youth.' But David said to Saul, 'Your servant used to keep sheep for his father; and whenever a lion or a bear came, and took a lamb from the flock, I went after it and struck it down, rescuing the lamb from its mouth; and if it turned against me, I would catch it by the jaw, strike it down, and kill it. Your servant has killed both lions and bears; and this uncircumcised Philistine shall be like one of them, since he has defied the armies of the living God.' David said, 'The LORD, who saved me from the paw of the lion and from the paw of the bear, will save me from the hand of this Philistine.' So Saul said to David, 'Go, and may the LORD be with you!' Saul clothed David with his armor; he put a bronze helmet on his head and clothed him with a coat of mail. David strapped Saul's sword over the armor, and he tried in vain to walk, for he was not used to them. Then David said to Saul, 'I cannot walk with these; for I am not used to them.' So David removed them. Then he took his staff in his hand, and chose five smooth stones from the wadi, and put them in his shepherd's bag, in the pouch; his sling was in his hand, and he drew near to the Philistine. The Philistine came on and drew near to David, with his shield-bearer in front of him. When the Philistine looked and saw David, he disdained him, for he was only a youth, ruddy and handsome in appearance. The Philistine said to David, 'Am I a dog, that you come to me with sticks?' And the Philistine cursed David by his gods. The Philistine said to David, 'Come to me, and I will give your flesh to the birds of the air and to the wild animals of the field.' But David said to the Philistine, 'You come to me with sword and spear and javelin; but I come to you in the name of the LORD of hosts, the God of the armies of Israel, whom you have defied. This very day the LORD will deliver you into my hand, and I will strike you down and cut off your head; and I will give the dead bodies of the Philistine army this very day to the birds of the air and to the wild animals of the earth, so that all the earth may know that there is a God in Israel, and that all this assembly may know that the LORD does not save by sword and spear; for the battle is the LORD's and he will give you into our hand.' When the Philistine drew nearer to meet David, David ran quickly toward the battle line to meet the Philistine. David put his hand in his bag, took out a stone, slung it, and struck the Philistine on his forehead; the stone sank into his forehead, and he fell face down on the ground. So David prevailed over the Philistine with a sling and a stone, striking down the Philistine and killing him; there was no sword in David's hand. Then David ran and stood over the Philistine; he grasped his sword, drew it out of its sheath, and killed him; then he cut off his head with it. When the Philistines saw that their champion was dead, they fled."

19. *2 Samuel 1:25–26*. "How the mighty have fallen in the midst of the battle! Jonathan lies slain upon your high places. I am distressed for you, my brother Jonathan; greatly beloved were you to me; your love to me was wonderful, passing the love of women."

20. *2 Samuel 11:14–17*. "In the morning David wrote a letter to Joab, and sent it by the hand of Uriah. In the letter he wrote, 'Set Uriah in the forefront of the hardest fighting, and then draw back from him, so that he may be struck down and die.' As Joab was besieging the city, he assigned Uriah to the place where he knew there were valiant warriors. The men of the city came out and fought with Joab; and some of the servants of David among the people fell. Uriah the Hittite was killed as well."

21. *2 Samuel 11:2*. "It happened, late one afternoon, when David rose from his couch and was walking about on the roof of the king's house, that he saw from the roof a woman bathing; the woman was very beautiful."

22. *1 Kings 17:8–16*. "Then the word of the LORD came to him, saying, 'Go now to Zarephath, which belongs to Sidon, and live there; for I have commanded a widow there

to feed you.' So he set out and went to Zarephath. When he came to the gate of the town, a widow was there gathering sticks; he called to her and said, 'Bring me a little water in a vessel, so that I may drink.' As she was going to bring it, he called to her and said, 'Bring me a morsel of bread in your hand.' But she said, 'As the LORD your God lives, I have nothing baked, only a handful of meal in a jar, and a little oil in a jug; I am now gathering a couple of sticks, so that I may go home and prepare it for myself and my son, that we may eat it, and die.' Elijah said to her, 'Do not be afraid; go and do as you have said; but first make me a little cake of it and bring it to me, and afterwards make something for yourself and your son. For thus says the LORD the God of Israel: The jar of meal will not be emptied and the jug of oil will not fail until the day that the LORD sends rain on the earth.' She went and did as Elijah said, so that she as well as he and her household ate for many days. The jar of meal was not emptied, neither did the jug of oil fail, according to the word of the LORD that he spoke by Elijah."

23. *1 Kings 17:3–6.* "'Go from here and turn eastward, and hide yourself by the Wadi Cherith, which is east of the Jordan. You shall drink from the wadi, and I have commanded the ravens to feed you there.' So he went and did according to the word of the LORD; he went and lived by the Wadi Cherith, which is east of the Jordan. The ravens brought him bread and meat in the morning, and bread and meat in the evening; and he drank from the wadi."

24. *2 Kings 2:1–14.* "Now when the LORD was about to take Elijah up to heaven by a whirlwind, Elijah and Elisha were on their way from Gilgal. Elijah said to Elisha, 'Stay here; for the LORD has sent me as far as Bethel.' But Elisha said, 'As the LORD lives, and as you yourself live, I will not leave you.' So they went down to Bethel. The company of prophets who were in Bethel came out to Elisha, and said to him, 'Do you know that today the LORD will take your master away from you?' And he said, 'Yes, I know; keep silent.'

Elijah said to him, 'Elisha, stay here; for the LORD has sent me to Jericho.' But he said, 'As the LORD lives, and as you yourself live, I will not leave you.' So they came to Jericho. The company of prophets who were at Jericho drew near to Elisha, and said to him, 'Do you know that today the LORD will take your master away from you?' And he answered, 'Yes, I know; be silent.' Then Elijah said to him, 'Stay here; for the LORD has sent me to the Jordan.' But he said, 'As the LORD lives, and as you yourself live, I will not leave you.' So the two of them went on. Fifty men of the company of prophets also went, and stood at some distance from them, as they both were standing by the Jordan. Then Elijah took his mantle and rolled it up, and struck the water; the water was parted to the one side and to the other, until the two of them crossed on dry ground. When they had crossed, Elijah said to Elisha, 'Tell me what I may do for you, before I am taken from you.' Elisha said, 'Please let me inherit a double share of your spirit.' He responded, 'You have asked a hard thing; yet, if you see me as I am being taken from you, it will be granted you; if not, it will not.' As they continued walking and talking, a chariot of fire and horses of fire separated the two of them, and Elijah ascended in a whirlwind into heaven. Elisha kept watching and crying out, 'Father, father! The chariots of Israel and its horsemen!' But when he could no longer see him, he grasped his own clothes and tore them in two pieces."

25. *2 Kings 2:11*. "As they continued walking and talking, a chariot of fire and horses of fire separated the two of them, and Elijah ascended in a whirlwind into heaven."

26. *Genesis 16:1–16*. "Now Sarai, Abram's wife, bore him no children. She had an Egyptian slave-girl whose name was Hagar, and Sarai said to Abram, 'You see that the LORD has prevented me from bearing children; go in to my slave-girl; it may be that I shall obtain children by her.' And Abram listened to the voice of Sarai. So, after Abram had lived ten years in the land of Canaan, Sarai, Abram's wife,

took Hagar the Egyptian, her slave-girl, and gave her to her husband Abram as a wife. He went in to Hagar, and she conceived; and when she saw that she had conceived, she looked with contempt on her mistress. Then Sarai said to Abram, 'May the wrong done to me be on you! I gave my slave-girl to your embrace, and when she saw that she had conceived, she looked on me with contempt. May the LORD judge between you and me!' But Abram said to Sarai, 'Your slave-girl is in your power; do to her as you please.' Then Sarai dealt harshly with her, and she ran away from her. The angel of the LORD found her by a spring of water in the wilderness, the spring on the way to Shur. And he said, 'Hagar, slave-girl of Sarai, where have you come from and where are you going?' She said, 'I am running away from my mistress Sarai.' The angel of the LORD said to her, 'Return to your mistress, and submit to her.' The angel of the LORD also said to her, 'I will so greatly multiply your offspring that they cannot be counted for multitude.' And the angel of the LORD said to her, 'Now you have conceived and shall bear a son; you shall call him Ishmael, for the LORD has given heed to your affliction. He shall be a wild ass of a man, with his hand against everyone, and everyone's hand against him; and he shall live at odds with all his kin.' So she named the LORD who spoke to her, 'You are El-roi'; for she said, 'Have I really seen God and remained alive after seeing him?' Therefore the well was called Beer-lahai-roi; it lies between Kadesh and Bered. Hagar bore Abram a son; and Abram named his son, whom Hagar bore, Ishmael. Abram was eighty-six years old when Hagar bore him Ishmael."

27. *Genesis 17:23–27.* "Then Abraham took his son Ishmael and all the slaves born in his house or bought with his money, every male among the men of Abraham's house, and he circumcised the flesh of their foreskins that very day, as God had said to him. Abraham was ninety-nine years old when he was circumcised in the flesh of his fore-

skin. And his son Ishmael was thirteen years old when he was circumcised in the flesh of his foreskin. That very day Abraham and his son Ishmael were circumcised; and all the men of his house, slaves born in the house and those bought with money from a foreigner, were circumcised with him."

28. *Genesis 18:1–15.* "The LORD appeared to Abraham by the oaks of Mamre, as he sat at the entrance of his tent in the heat of the day. He looked up and saw three men standing near him. When he saw them, he ran from the tent entrance to meet them, and bowed down to the ground. He said, 'My lord, if I find favor with you, do not pass by your servant. Let a little water be brought, and wash your feet, and rest yourselves under the tree. Let me bring a little bread, that you may refresh yourselves, and after that you may pass on—since you have come to your servant.' So they said, 'Do as you have said.' And Abraham hastened into the tent to Sarah, and said, 'Make ready quickly three measures of choice flour, knead it, and make cakes.' Abraham ran to the herd, and took a calf, tender and good, and gave it to the servant, who hastened to prepare it. Then he took curds and milk and the calf that he had prepared, and set it before them; and he stood by them under the tree while they ate. They said to him, 'Where is your wife Sarah?' And he said, 'There, in the tent.' Then one said, 'I will surely return to you in due season, and your wife Sarah shall have a son.' And Sarah was listening at the tent entrance behind him. Now Abraham and Sarah were old, advanced in age; it had ceased to be with Sarah after the manner of women. So Sarah laughed to herself, saying, 'After I have grown old, and my husband is old, shall I have pleasure?' The LORD said to Abraham, 'Why did Sarah laugh, and say, "Shall I indeed bear a child, now that I am old?" Is anything too wonderful for the LORD? At the set time I will return to you, in due season, and Sarah shall have a son.' But Sarah

denied, saying, 'I did not laugh'; for she was afraid. He said, 'Oh yes, you did laugh.'"

29. *Genesis 21:8–19.* "The child grew, and was weaned; and Abraham made a great feast on the day that Isaac was weaned. But Sarah saw the son of Hagar the Egyptian, whom she had borne to Abraham, playing with her son Isaac. So she said to Abraham, 'Cast out this slave woman with her son; for the son of this slave woman shall not inherit along with my son Isaac.' The matter was very distressing to Abraham on account of his son. But God said to Abraham, 'Do not be distressed because of the boy and because of your slave woman; whatever Sarah says to you, do as she tells you, for it is through Isaac that offspring shall be named for you. As for the son of the slave woman, I will make a nation of him also, because he is your offspring.' So Abraham rose early in the morning, and took bread and a skin of water, and gave it to Hagar, putting it on her shoulder, along with the child, and sent her away. And she departed, and wandered about in the wilderness of Beer-sheba. When the water in the skin was gone, she cast the child under one of the bushes. Then she went and sat down opposite him a good way off, about the distance of a bowshot; for she said, 'Do not let me look on the death of the child.' And as she sat opposite him, she lifted up her voice and wept. And God heard the voice of the boy; and the angel of God called to Hagar from heaven, and said to her, 'What troubles you, Hagar? Do not be afraid; for God has heard the voice of the boy where he is. Come, lift up the boy and hold him fast with your hand, for I will make a great nation of him.' Then God opened her eyes and she saw a well of water. She went, and filled the skin with water, and gave the boy a drink."

30. *Genesis 21:17–21.* "And God heard the voice of the boy; and the angel of God called to Hagar from heaven, and said to her, 'What troubles you, Hagar? Do not be afraid; for God has heard the voice of the boy where he is. Come,

lift up the boy and hold him fast with your hand, for I will make a great nation of him.' Then God opened her eyes and she saw a well of water. She went, and filled the skin with water, and gave the boy a drink. God was with the boy, and he grew up; he lived in the wilderness, and became an expert with the bow. He lived in the wilderness of Paran; and his mother got a wife for him from the land of Egypt."

31. *Matthew 1:21.* "She will bear a son, and you are to name him Jesus, for he will save his people from their sins."

32. *Hosea 4:6.* "My people are destroyed for lack of knowledge; because you have rejected knowledge, I reject you from being a priest to me. And since you have forgotten the law of your God, I also will forget your children."

33. *Perdition.* A noun. In ancient traditions: the netherworld; the abode of the dead; a place of final spiritual ruin.

34. *John 17:22–23.* "The glory that you have given me I have given them, so that they may be one, as we are one, I in them and you in me, that they may become completely one, so that the world may know that you have sent me and have loved them even as you have loved me."

35. *Matthew 10:2–4.* "These are the names of the twelve apostles: first, Simon, also known as Peter, and his brother Andrew; James son of Zebedee, and his brother John; Philip and Bartholomew; Thomas and Matthew the tax collector; James son of Alphaeus, and Thaddaeus; Simon the Cananaean, and Judas Iscariot, the one who betrayed him."

36. *Luke 6:31.* "Do to others as you would have them do to you."

37. *Acts 1:8.* "But you will receive power when the Holy Spirit has come upon you; and you will be my witnesses in Jerusalem, in all Judea and Samaria, and to the ends of the earth."

38. *John 20:1–18.* "Early on the first day of the week, while it was still dark, Mary Magdalene came to the tomb and saw

that the stone had been removed from the tomb. So she ran and went to Simon Peter and the other disciple, the one whom Jesus loved, and said to them, 'They have taken the Lord out of the tomb, and we do not know where they have laid him.' Then Peter and the other disciple set out and went toward the tomb. The two were running together, but the other disciple outran Peter and reached the tomb first. He bent down to look in and saw the linen wrappings lying there, but he did not go in. Then Simon Peter came, following him, and went into the tomb. He saw the linen wrappings lying there, and the cloth that had been on Jesus' head, not lying with the linen wrappings but rolled up in a place by itself. Then the other disciple, who reached the tomb first, also went in, and he saw and believed; for as yet they did not understand the scripture, that he must rise from the dead. Then the disciples returned to their homes. But Mary stood weeping outside the tomb. As she wept, she bent over to look into the tomb; and she saw two angels in white, sitting where the body of Jesus had been lying, one at the head and the other at the feet. They said to her, 'Woman, why are you weeping?' She said to them, 'They have taken away my Lord, and I do not know where they have laid him.' When she had said this, she turned around and saw Jesus standing there, but she did not know that it was Jesus. Jesus said to her, 'Woman, why are you weeping? Whom are you looking for?' Supposing him to be the gardener, she said to him, 'Sir, if you have carried him away, tell me where you have laid him, and I will take him away.' Jesus said to her, 'Mary!' She turned and said to him in Hebrew, 'Rabbouni!' (which means Teacher). Jesus said to her, 'Do not hold on to me, because I have not yet ascended to the Father. But go to my brothers and say to them, "I am ascending to my Father and your Father, to my God and your God."' Mary Magdalene went and announced to the disciples, 'I have seen the Lord'; and she told them that he had said these things to her."

39. *Matthew 28:18–20.* "And Jesus came and said to them, 'All authority in heaven and on earth has been given to me. Go therefore and make disciples of all nations, baptizing them in the name of the Father and of the Son and of the Holy Spirit, and teaching them to obey everything that I have commanded you. And remember, I am with you always, to the end of the age.'"

40. *John 16:13–15.* "When the Spirit of truth comes, he will guide you into all the truth; for he will not speak on his own, but will speak whatever he hears, and he will declare to you the things that are to come. He will glorify me, because he will take what is mine and declare it to you. All that the Father has is mine. For this reason I said that he will take what is mine and declare it to you."

ABOUT THE AUTHOR

With a degree from Iowa State University in hand, Larry Moeller entered corporate America and climbed the ladder to a divisional general manager role. After twenty years of increasing sales and management responsibility, he founded a small business and, for over two decades, has helped client companies across North America fulfill their mission by identifying, attracting, and retaining exceptional talent.

Financial security provided by this small business has opened the door to bivocational calls in Christian ministry, including several years as lay pastor/developer for a struggling inner-city church in Sacramento, California. Believing that it takes a church to raise a village, his passion is helping a ministry reengage with its neighborhood.

Sometime around age forty, God placed this call on my heart as the core of my life purpose:

> To help those who have yet to know Jesus
> come to know him…and for those who do know
> him, to come to know him more deeply.

This purpose has been a gift and has helped clarify the competing demands on my time. Whether in matters of faith or family, vocation or volunteerism, writing or leisure, if the dots connect back to this purpose, then I trust it is of God. If the dots lead away from that purpose, it's time to rethink and recalibrate.

The books I've been privileged to write—the earlier Claim the Flame and The Query, together with the most recent A Fateful Flaw—are the result of connecting the dots. In the exercise of writing them, I have come to know God in Jesus more deeply. Through them, may you as well.

Larry Moeller
querier@risenindeed.com

CPSIA information can be obtained
at www.ICGtesting.com
Printed in the USA
BVHW081119090822
644142BV00005B/255